A DARING PLAN

My plan was right there, all of it, coming right at me. What I was seeing was getting better every second. I looked at my aunt and uncle, wondering if they were aware of what I was thinking. But they weren't. The girl I'd met at the travel agency had given me her New York number and as soon as I got there I'd call her. She'd said she'd help.

Would I have gone if I'd known what was going to happen? I've asked myself that question an awful lot of times.

Sometimes I think I hear my name

AN AVON FLARE BOOK

Grateful acknowledgment is made to Jerry Vogel Music Company, Inc.,
for permission to reprint an excerpt from the lyrics to *Meet Me in St.
Louis, Louis* by F. A. Mills and Andrew B. Sterling. Copyright MCMXXI
by F. A. Mills and Andrew B. Sterling. Copyright assigned MCMXXXV
to Jerry Vogel Music Co. All rights reserved. International Copyright Se-
cured. Used by permission.

AVON BOOKS
A division of
The Hearst Corporation
1350 Avenue of the Americas
New York, New York 10019

· · ·

Tuesday

It began in St. Louis. St. Louis, says the almanac, has 448,649 people; is 61 square miles in area; has the biggest shoe company in the United States; and was named after a French king. But the most important thing for me last spring was that it's almost a thousand miles from the city of New York.

Not that New York City is *that* important. But it is where I was born, and where I lived with my parents before I lived in St. Louis. I live in St. Louis now. My parents live in New York. Both of them. But not together.

They got divorced. I don't know why. I'm not sure I want to. Besides, that's not what this is all about. The point is, when they got divorced they decided that what I needed was a good, regular home with two grown-ups living regular lives in regular ways, doing regular things. So, when I was about nine, I came to St. Louis to live with my regular Uncle Carl and my regular Aunt Lu. Aunt Lu is my mom's sister.

For the first three years I saw my folks pretty often, maybe four, five times a year. In between, there were letters, phone calls, presents. The next Easter—which was last year—I saw them in New York. I was supposed to go again last summer, but the only time I could have gone was when Uncle Carl could get me into this great scout camp.

I went to camp.

At Thanksgiving, Aunt Lu wasn't feeling too good, so I stayed home to help out while Uncle Carl was at a meeting. And at Christmas Uncle Carl decided we should go to Florida for Aunt Lu's health, which we did.

So, I didn't get to see my parents at Christmas. Also, for Christmas my dad sent me this huge model of a spaceship, and my mother sent records, records of corny band music. It was the presents that really upset me. I just wasn't into those things at all. I felt as if—since I hadn't seen my folks for so long—they didn't know me anymore.

That was scary.

I began to think that something was wrong. I felt I had to be with them alone, without my aunt or uncle standing by the phone or reading over my letters for spelling mistakes.

Not that I said anything. I was afraid to, afraid to upset things. And my aunt and uncle got upset very easily. They were always nervous about me, about how I felt, worried I might get angry at them. 'Specially my aunt. So I had to protect them, take care of them. Mostly I did it by not saying what was on my mind.

So, I didn't say or do anything about my parents. I did think about them, a lot. And I got more and more worried, 'specially since I was getting fewer and fewer letters and phone calls. I just didn't know what was going on.

Finally, spring vacation was close—and I had always gone East then. I was really looking forward to visiting New York. I just *had* to see my folks. Then my aunt and uncle announced that instead of going to New York, as soon as school was out I'd be going to England for spring vacation.

England!

"What if I don't want to go?" I said that morning in St. Louis. I said it quietly, almost as if it didn't matter.

"How could you *not* want to go?" cried Aunt Lu as she swirled the orange juice. "It's the chance of a lifetime, honey."

"I'll more than likely get other chances," I suggested.

"Now, honey," Aunt Lu said with one of her big smiles. "How many boys thirteen years of age have the opportunity to visit a foreign country? I wish *I* could go see Cousin Philip and the children."

"I never saw them before," I protested.

"They are family, Conrad, not strangers. Besides, you're so easygoing, you get along with everyone. Those're two of your blessings. He'll have a fine time, won't he, dear?" she said, asking help from Uncle Carl.

"It should be fun," he offered. "Meeting part of your family you've never seen. And England's very interesting, Conrad. Marvelous history, great tradition . . ."

I put on my listening look. When he seemed to be done, really done (I was never quite sure), all I said was, "I'd still rather visit my mom and dad."

They looked at me, they looked at each other, but they didn't say anything.

"I haven't seen them for almost a year," I said. "My dad told me that the next time I came he'd take me to the top of the Empire State Building."

Aunt Lu eyed Uncle Carl, which is a way they sometimes talk. He clasped his hands (a bad sign), leaned forward (a worse one), and said, "Aren't you happy here, Conrad?" He even tried to make a joke. "Isn't the Gateway Arch good enough for you?"

Somehow they had gotten it into their heads that if I talked about my parents, that meant I was unhappy. I was sorry I had said anything.

"Is something bothering you here?" Uncle Carl continued. "There's nothing you need, is there?" Where Aunt Lu was always hugging, he was always worried about *things*. And in his

4

way, he was generous. But what could I tell him—that having the right things didn't necessarily make me feel right? I couldn't. He would have been insulted. So again, I said nothing.

"We're only trying to help you have a good vacation," he said. "A special one. You must know that."

"Sure, I know," I said, and I meant it. But I don't think it came out sounding right.

Aunt Lu snuck up from behind and lassoed me with a hug. "Conrad," she said, "it's just this one short vacation, and a wonderful opportunity."

"When I was your age," added Uncle Carl, "I would have gone through tornados for the chance. As I see it, it doesn't make much sense for Conrad Murray to even suggest he's unhappy."

"I never said I was unhappy, Uncle Carl. I only said that during spring vacation I'd like to see my mom and dad."

Then Aunt Lu dropped a bomb on me. "You know, when this first came up, I spoke to your mother."

"What did she say?" I said, taken by surprise.

"She said it was a wonderful idea for you to visit your English cousins. Though she did so *desperately* want to see you, she *would* not, *could* not, stand in your way. She envies you, Conrad, positively *envies* you."

"She say anything for me?" I asked.

"How *stupid* of me," cried Aunt Lu. "She sent

all her love." And to prove it, Aunt Lu hung another hug around my neck.

"Anything else?" I wanted to know.

"She expressly said to remind you to send her a postcard from Buckingham Palace when you see the queen."

"Perhaps," said Uncle Carl as he stood up— meaning the discussion was over—"perhaps you won't fully appreciate such an adventure now. But when you look back on it, Conrad, you'll be glad you went."

There it was, then—I was going to England. As far as I could see, there was no way I'd be able to get to New York.

But I did.

I finished my breakfast, tore upstairs, made my bed properly, and checked that my room was okay, with everything neat, the way Aunt Lu liked it.

Leaving my school stuff parked by the door, I took out the garbage, then went back to the kitchen for my lunch. Aunt Lu was there, alone, wrapping up an apology-size piece of chocolate cake.

"Conrad," she said, her voice sort of mournful, "you do understand, don't you?"

Before I had time to figure out what it was I was supposed to understand, she told me, as always.

"Conrad," she said, "when your mother, my baby sister, and your father, who is a *fine* man,

6

came to a parting of the ways, being most un-happy and unsuitable for each other, they wanted most of all for you to have a stable, happy home. Your Uncle Carl and I, though we were older, without children of our own, wanted *so much* to do everything that was the best for you. The *best*, Conrad. It was your mother and father, *both* of them, who asked us to have you here. You do know that, don't you?"

"Sure," I said. I had heard it enough times to know how to handle it.

"Well, then . . . sometimes I think you forget all that," she let me know.

"I'm sorry," I said, and I really was sorry. Aunt Lu was so easy to hurt. She couldn't stand even a hint that she wasn't making me incredibly happy.

"Then, honey," she said, "about this trip to England we've arranged . . ."

I knew what to say. "Don't worry," I told her. "I'll go. And I promise I'll have a great time."

She felt so good about that, she gave me an-other hug. "The point is, Conrad," she said, "your mother's hours are crazier than ever. There wouldn't be anything for you to *do* in New York while she was at work. Same for your fa-ther, though I don't guess I know where he works these days."

"He runs Macy's department store," I told her.

"Well, I don't think he *runs* it, Conrad. Any-way, honey, the whole idea is for you to have an exciting, interesting vacation. Now, isn't that right?"

I took my usual way out: I nodded.

"Good," she said. "Now give me a kiss, say you love me, and off you go."

"Sure, Aunt Lu," I said, and I gave her the kiss she wanted. Then I ran out and caught my bus. I didn't *say* I loved her. I guess I did. But asking someone to say they love you—and she always asked—is like buying yourself a birthday present. It's more than likely exactly what you want. But it must make you feel awfully sad to get it.

On the bus I sat next to my friend Rick, who's in the same grade as me. He could hardly wait till I sat down. The minute I did, he said, "Guess what I'm doing over vacation?"

"What?"

"My folks got basketball play-off tickets," he announced. "Two games. What are you doing? Going to see your folks?"

I looked out the window. He wasn't trying to be mean or anything. But I couldn't explain. I mean, I wasn't even sure myself what was happening, really happening. So the easiest thing to do was say something he'd like to hear—something big.

I said, "You know my parents are actors, right?"

He nodded, yes, because that's what I had told him before.

"Well, they're going to act for the Queen of

8

England. Buckingham Palace. They want me to be there, so I figured I'd go."

"Is that true?" he asked.

"I just said it, didn't I?"

"When?"

"Friday after next," I said. "Spring vacation. Just like that. Off to England to see the queen."

He believed it. And when word got around school, I scored some points. But in my head I was still trying to find a way *not* to go.

Two days later I was sure I had found it.

· · ·

Thursday

This is what happened. I was supposed to stop at a travel agency on the way home from school to pick up my tickets for England. It was a big building—flags from lots of countries out front, a whole bunch of travel agents inside. Uncle Carl always chooses the best.

"Can I help you?" a woman asked when I went in.

"I was told to ask for Barbara Stone," I said. "I have to pick up some tickets."

"She's busy with a client right now," the woman said. "Why don't you have a seat over there?" She nodded toward four red plush seats. Two people were already there, a girl with a magazine and an old guy reading a newspaper. I sat down between them and settled in for a long wait. I was worried about the time. I had played ball at school before coming to the travel agency, and I was supposed to be home by five-thirty.

On one wall was a row of eight clocks, each one showing a different time from a different place, New York around the world to China. Naturally, the only clock they didn't have was one showing St. Louis time—the time I needed to know.

I turned to the old guy and said, "Do you know what time it is in St. Louis?"

Either he didn't hear me or he didn't want to answer. He never stopped reading.

"It's four-twenty," said the girl. I hadn't even asked her.

"Thanks," I said, looking at her closely for the first time.

She was wearing some kind of uniform—blue plaid skirt, green jacket, white blouse, black tie, and a hat made from the same stuff as her skirt.

Though I couldn't tell for sure, I guessed she was about my age. Her face was plain; mouth small, thin; eyes masked by eyeglasses with plain pink frames. Her hair was straight, black, cut just below her ears. There was a tiny teddy bear pin on the collar of her blouse. At first she seemed very ordinary.

But the more I looked at her the stranger she seemed. It wasn't that she was out of place—she just didn't seem to be part of anything. I mean, she didn't look comfortable, or uncomfortable—just not attached. Still, she had obviously heard me ask the time, because she had answered.

"Been waiting long?" I said, feeling that I ought to whisper.

She looked up at me. "They are getting my ticket." Her eyes were strange, too, distant, not seeing me.

"Where you going?" I said, wanting to make conversation.

"New York," she said.

"Fantastic," I said. "Best place in the world."

She said nothing, only went back to her reading.

"I have to go to England," I said after a moment.

"I'd like to go there sometime," she said, still not looking at me. "They say it's very beautiful."

Her politeness, the way she talked, puzzled me. She didn't seem to mean what she was saying. She acted as if she didn't really want to talk at all. I thought, *Maybe she's a zombie.*

"New York is nicer," I tried.

For just a flicker those eyes turned real, like they belonged to something alive that was peering from a cave. In that second I got the notion that something was wrong, very wrong.

"My parents live there," I went on.

I figured she'd ask me something about my parents or say something about hers. Instead, she went back to her magazine as if I wasn't there.

It was then that I noticed something I'll never

forget. It was on her hand, her right hand, on the back, so tiny that I almost didn't see it at all. It was a tattoo, a little picture of a butterfly, green, so unlike all the rest of her that it startled me. See, everything else was right, prim, proper, just the way it was supposed to be. But that— that tiny thing was, well, wild. I had the feeling that it was more important than anything else I was seeing. A clue—but to what I didn't know.

Bending forward, I looked to see what she was reading. It was *True Romances*. On the cover was a picture of a lady, partly undressed, smoking a bent cigarette and looking very sleepy.

"Do you live around here?" I asked, getting more and more curious.

"I live in New York. I only go to school here," she said softly. "The St. Agnes Academy for Girls. I like it very much," she added, though I hadn't asked. "The sisters are nice."

"How come you go to school here if you live in New York?" I wanted to know.

"St. Agnes is one of the country's best schools," she explained, sounding like she was reading from an advertisement.

"Sure," I said. "But wouldn't you rather be in New York?"

For a minute she didn't say anything. Finally she said, "It's better here."

Just then a woman came over to us.

"Miss Sperling?" she said.

"Yes, ma'am," said the girl, standing right up.

13

"If you'll come with me, your ticket is ready."

The girl started to follow, but to my surprise she stopped to say, "Have a pleasant trip to England."

I watched as she got her ticket, shook hands with the travel agent, and went out. The next surprise was to see her march up to this huge black car. A man in a uniform and cap got out and held the back door open for her.

Then I saw that she had left her *True Romances*. Grabbing it, I ran after her, but I was too late. The car had pulled away.

When I went back inside I was told I could pick up my tickets.

"Oh, yes, the boy who's going to England," said Miss Stone. She opened a drawer and handed me an envelope. "First class all the way. Your parents certainly are treating you right. Have a nice trip."

"Thanks," I said. Then I just stood there. That girl was stuck in my mind. There was something really weird about her. And I tried to figure out what it was about her that was bugging me. Then it hit me: *She didn't want to go to New York.*

"Do you know where the St. Agnes Academy for Girls is?" I asked the agent quickly.

"It's a couple of miles out on Medford Avenue," she said. "On a big estate. Very exclusive school."

I stuffed the tickets and the *True Romances*

magazine into my book bag and hurried to catch a bus home.

I was sure I had just figured out a way to get to New York.

. . .

Friday

"My, look at you this morning!" cried Aunt Lu when I came down to breakfast wearing a dress shirt, tie, good trousers, good shoes, and my going-out jacket. "What's the occasion, honey?"

Uncle Carl, peering over his newspaper, smiled. "You look like you're going courting," he said.

"We have a special assembly in school," I told them.

When I went up to my room to get my school stuff, I carefully placed the copy of *True Romances* in my book bag. The night before I had wrapped it fancy. It was going to be my ticket to St. Agnes and that girl.

On the bus, Rick wanted to know why I was dressed up. I said, "I've got to get into practice wearing clothes like this. Visiting the queen and all. It's expected."

After school I got to the St. Agnes Academy without trouble. It seemed more like a resort hotel than a school, in what looked like a huge park with trees and enough grass for sixteen soccer fields.

Before reaching the main entrance, I took out the giftwrapped magazine and stashed my book bag under a bush. Then I went up to this uniformed guy who was sitting in a little house by the main driveway.

"I'm here to see Miss Sperling," I announced. "She's a student."

"She expecting you?" the guard asked, checking over his clipboard.

"Not exactly," I said. I had my story all prepared. "See, I'm her brother, and since it's her birthday I thought I'd surprise her. I brought a gift," I said, showing him the package.

He actually smiled. "Now that's what I call pleasant and decent," he said, no longer stiff. "Certainly don't want to announce you, then."

"No, sir, it's a surprise."

"Surprise it will be. Find your own way?"

"Oh, sure. Been here lots of times."

"Thought you looked familiar. Come on through."

I went right to the biggest building. By the big double doors was a metal plaque with the name of the school on it. I knocked softly.

In a few moments one of the doors swung open and a face peered out. It was just a face, too, because it was a nun, her eyes, mouth, and nose framed in a white headpiece that hid her hair and ears.

"Yes?" she said.

"I've come to see Miss Sperling." It came out in a whisper.

She looked at me blankly.

"I was just passing through St. Louis," I said carefully. "From New York. Her parents asked me to deliver a gift." That was the second story I had worked out.

She looked at me with a puzzled expression.

"I had my car wait at the gate," I continued to lie. "I didn't know if it was right to bring it in. Her parents did send this gift. . . . "

"I see," she said at last. "Please come in." She held the door open.

It was as grand inside as it was out. Everything was made of wood, dark wood, except the floor, which was stone. On one wall was a statue of Jesus on the Cross. Opposite, kneeling, was Mary.

"What is your name, please?" the nun asked.

"Conrad Buckingham," I told her. The fake last name just slipped out. I guess I was thinking about England. "I flew in today."

"Please wait here," she said. With a swirl of her white habit she hurried down the hallway and disappeared. Waiting, I kept my eyes away from the Jesus and Mary statues. I don't believe in Hell, but I was in the wrong place to try my luck. I was glad when the white-robed nun came back.

"Sister Mary would like to see you first," she said.

She took me to a small room off the main hallway. It was like any other office I'd ever seen—books, file cabinet, typewriter, all the usual stuff—except for a religious picture on the wall. Seated behind the desk was another, older nun. She was all in white, too, but I saw this wisp of gray hair sticking out over her forehead and it made me feel better.

"Sister Mary," said the nun who had let me in, "this is the young man who has come from New York to see Miss Sperling." Then she left the room.

"Won't you please sit down," Sister Mary said softly, looking me right in the eye. She had a nice face. In fact, I almost decided to just tell her the truth, but by then I was afraid to. So instead, I tried to guess what she was thinking, and to figure out what she'd want me to say.

"Conrad Buckingham," she said, still watching me. "An unexpected visit."

"Right," I said, making up new details as I went on. "I was passing through on the way to California. Hollywood. My parents are movie actors. They only make G-rated films—for Disney. Her parents and mine are good friends. They asked me to bring her something," I said, lifting my package.

"That was putting you to a great deal of trouble," said Sister Mary, looking at me searchingly.

"We're old friends," I said, only wishing I knew the girl's first name.

"I don't recall her parents ever doing such a thing before," said Sister Mary. "Nancy hears from them with great punctuality."

Nancy. I hung on to the name.

"You do know Nancy is going home in a few days, don't you?" she went on carefully. "Her parents insist that as soon as there is a break she go right home. So devoted." She leaned forward slightly, as if she expected me to agree with her. At the same time the way she kept looking at me made me feel sure she suspected something. But then she said, "I have asked Nancy to come along. Certainly you can have a few minutes. I do wish it could be more. But dinner will be served shortly, and I can't ask you to stay."

Rising from her chair, she went to a side door, opened it, and called, "Nancy, come in, dear. Here's a surprise. It's your friend Conrad Buckingham. He's just come from New York."

Nancy, dressed in her school uniform, walked in, looking really puzzled.

I stood up and gave it my best. "Hi, Nancy!"

She was too baffled to say anything. Luckily, Sister Mary was standing behind her, beaming at us. "Nancy, don't forget. Dinner soon," she said. With a final smile, she left the two of us alone.

* * *

I suppose the whole thing sounds like it's supposed to be funny. I guess, up to that point, it was. Real TV stuff. But as soon as we were alone, all that vanished. Right away I could see that Nancy Sperling was frightened, frightened of me.

"I don't know you," she whispered.

"Sure you do," I insisted. "Remember? You were at the travel agent's yesterday getting a ticket for New York. We talked there."

The look on her face told me that my explanation only made her more nervous. "Sister Mary said you just came from New York."

For a second I thought of making up another story. But then I decided I'd try the truth. I had nothing to lose. "I only said that so I could speak to you," I told her.

"What do you want?" she asked.

I took a deep breath and finally said what I'd come to say, spilled my great idea. "You said you were going to New York, right? And I told you I was going to England, remember? But I had this feeling that you didn't want to go to New York, that you'd rather go to England."

She became pale. "I never said that," she said, her voice very small.

"Right, you didn't *say* it," I agreed. "But it felt like it. Now, look, I don't want to go to England. I want to go to New York. The point is, I had this idea that we could, well, switch tickets. Nobody has to know. That way you could go where you wanted and so could I."

21

"I don't understand what you're talking about," she said, looking at me as if I had escaped from the local loony bin.

"I want to go to New York," I said. "Badly."

"Why don't you?"

"I can't."

"Why?"

The truth wasn't working. I switched back to a story. "My parents live in New York," I began. "They're fantastically rich. They're afraid I might be kidnapped and held for ransom. So I live here with my aunt and uncle. And *they* don't want me to visit my parents."

She still looked puzzled.

"See," I said, "jealous of all that money. And they get part of it for taking care of me. They're afraid I might not come back."

"Would you?"

"I don't know," I admitted.

For a second I thought she knew I wasn't telling the truth, and I thought she'd say something. Instead, she just looked at the floor. I hadn't the slightest idea what she was thinking. But when she lifted her head it was my turn to be upset. Because on her face was nothing but pain, pain all over.

"I'm sorry," she managed to say. "I can't do it."

The way she said it—that look she had— didn't leave any room for me to argue. It was final. She meant it and I knew it. Right away I gave up the whole notion of trading tickets. I

know it must seem crazy, but I had really believed my great plan was going to work.

Suddenly she said, "I have my own phone in
New York. I could call your parents if you'd like
me to. I'll tell them you want to see them."

I felt sick. "No, no thanks," I got out. I guess
I had built my hopes up high, higher than I'd
realized. But as my spirits sank, hers seemed to
rise.

"My father is an important lawyer," she said.
"Maybe he could help you."

I felt like one of those flattened beer cans you
see on the road, crushed and empty. But I just
said, "That's okay."

"It's no problem," she said earnestly, as if she
had to make up for not doing what I wanted.
"I'll ask my father. I'm fairly certain that when
I'm in New York I'll see my parents. I'll talk to
them about you."

That zapped me. "Didn't you say you were
going home to New York?" I said.

"Yes."

"That Sister Mary was just telling me how
your parents always wanted you home."

She wouldn't look at me.

"Then how come," I persisted, "you only
might see your parents?"

"They need their privacy," she said softly but
matter-of-factly. "My sister and I have our own
apartment. It's in the same building where they
live."

"Are you serious?" I said, trying to decide if she was putting me on.

Instead of answering, she searched around on Sister Mary's desk until she found a pen and paper. She wrote out her New York phone number. "Don't be discouraged. If you'd like you may call me. I promise I'll try to help." She held out the scrap she had written on.

I had to take it. "No fooling," I said. "Do you really have your own apartment in New York?"

She said nothing.

"If you've got a place in New York," I tried, "how come you go to school here?"

She went back into that careful, zombie way she had. "It seems best," she answered.

I studied her, wishing I knew what was going on in her head. Then I suddenly remembered the package, my excuse for getting in to see her. "Hey," I said, "I did bring a present." I held out the wrapped magazine.

She was reluctant to take it.

"Go on, it's yours anyway."

She took it and slowly began to peel away the wrapping paper. The second she realized what it was her face turned absolutely crimson. She all but threw it back at me. "I can't have that here," she cried in a throaty whisper, really upset. "Please take it and go."

"I'm sorry," I said. "I thought you might have—" I stopped as Sister Mary, smiling, came back into the room.

"Time for dinner, Nancy."

24

Nancy couldn't get away fast enough—she almost ran from the room.

I saw that Sister Mary was puzzled, but all she said was, "Sister Teresa will see you out."

Sister Teresa, the first nun, walked me to the front door. "Did you forget to give Nancy the gift?" she suddenly asked, noticing that I was still holding the package.

"She didn't want it." It was the only thing I could say.

Holding the magazine in a tight roll, I collected my school stuff from under the bush and went home. On the way I don't know what I thought of most—trying to get out of the England trip, or Nancy Sperling. I mean, what I had seen and heard didn't fit together. In the first place, I was certain she didn't want to go home to New York. Still, she was going. Then, that Sister Mary had said her parents were so devoted to her. But Nancy had her own apartment; she didn't live with them, said she might not even see them. And that magazine. She had been reading it, but when I brought it back to her, she freaked out. Something was really upsetting her.

She was afraid of something—but what, I hadn't the slightest idea.

...

Wednesday

"Time to go over it all," said Uncle Carl. He had spread out all the papers connected with my trip in solitaire fashion on the table where my aunt did jigsaw puzzles. I was sitting opposite him and Aunt Lu was standing at my back.

"Excited?" she asked, giving me a hug.

"I guess so," I said, trying hard to give them what they wanted.

A whole week had passed and I still hadn't found a way out. I had just about given up.

"Here," began Uncle Carl, picking up a small blue book, "is your passport. *Very* important. You'll be asked to show it to various officials. They'll stamp it. Perfectly normal. Understand?"

"Yes."

"Addresses," he said, showing me a paper with addresses and phone numbers for my English cousins and for both my parents in New

York, *Right*, I thought. *That's where I want to be.* He had even put down our phone number in St. Louis.

"Here're your tickets," he said, holding them up. "Coming and going, all together in one booklet. When you get to London, give your return ticket directly to Cousin Philip, who will hold it for you. You don't want to lose it."

I was trying to act interested, but I wished it was all over with, including the vacation. I kept thinking, *Why can't they ever just let me do what I want?*

"Now," he continued, "let's review what will happen. Right after your lunch on Friday, we'll pick you up and drive directly to the airport. We'll have your suitcase. Once we get there, a stewardess will take care of you."

"I can take care of myself, Uncle Carl," I objected, wondering if I'd get even one second to be by myself.

"We know you can manage—it's the airline that insists," said Aunt Lu. I didn't believe her.

"Now," Uncle Carl went on, "when we turn you over to the stewardess, we'll have to leave. Don't be distressed. Perfectly normal. The flight to New York, by the way, will provide supper."

"Lots of good food, Conrad," said Aunt Lu.

It took maybe four seconds for it to hit me. "New York *City*?" I said. "I thought I was going to England."

"Of course. You only pass through New York," Uncle Carl explained. "Kennedy Airport.

27

Unfortunately, there are no nonstops from St. Louis to London. In New York, Conrad, you de-plane, and after a short stopover, you board the plane for England. You'll get to London at eight o'clock in the morning, their time. Pretty early, ours."

"Do try to get some sleep on the plane," urged Aunt Lu, patting my head.

Suddenly I was excited, beginning to see something fantastic, but trying not to show it. "Let me get this straight," I said, just to make sure. "I'm flying to New York City, getting off, then waiting, then going on another plane?"

"Correct," said Uncle Carl. "There's no need to be worried. Someone will be with you all the time. You'll be put on the right plane."

Worried! I was only worried that he would read my mind, because what I was seeing was getting better every second. "How much time between planes, Uncle Carl? Five minutes?"

It seemed to take forever for Uncle Carl to read the ticket. "One hour and forty minutes," he finally said. "Remember, the flight from St. Louis might be delayed. You might not have all that time. But, Conrad, I assure you, there's no chance of your missing connections. You won't be stranded, if that's what concerns you."

"Don't worry, honey," chimed in Aunt Lu. "Your Uncle Carl has it worked out to the last minute."

Worried? My plan was right there, all of it, coming right at me: how I would go as I was supposed to, but, once I got to New York, I'd take off, go into the city on my own, then to my parents. Of course, I couldn't go right to them. My aunt and uncle would check with my mom and dad first thing. What I had to do was make them think I was lost. That way I'd be in control.

I looked at them, wondering if they were aware of what I was thinking. But they weren't. They just went on fussing over those papers.

I couldn't get out of the living room fast enough.

As soon as I got to my room I pulled the *True Romances* magazine out from under my mattress. Inside the cover was the slip of paper on which Nancy Sperling had written her New York telephone number. I studied it, then carefully put it inside my wallet. That was the rest of my plan: as soon as I got to New York and was free, I'd call her. She'd said she'd help, and she had her own apartment—the perfect place to go while I was keeping out of sight.

When my lights were out, Aunt Lu slipped into my room. She sat down on the bed and squeezed my hand. "Only *think*, Conrad, this time on Friday you'll be flying high over the Atlantic Ocean. How I wish *I* could be going! Just think!"

I *was* thinking—not about any oceans, but about New York.

Would I have gone if I'd known what was going to happen? I've asked myself that question an awful lot of times.

. . .

Friday

As Uncle Carl had planned, they picked me up at school and on the way to the airport I put on a tie and jacket. By the time we got to the terminal, I was looking pretty much the same as I had on the day I went to the St. Agnes Academy.

After parking, Uncle Carl took my suitcase and led the way. Aunt Lu took my arm and kept squeezing it as we walked.

I checked in and got a window seat, and then we went to the security check. A flight attendant was there, looking neat and smiley. She introduced herself as Michelle.

"One final thing," Uncle Carl said to me. "We've asked Cousin Philip to have you call us when you arrive so we can rest easy. Never mind the time. Your Aunt Lu will fret if she doesn't hear from you. She'll think you're lost. You know her."

I sure did know. If I didn't call from England, they'd know fast that something was wrong. And, of course, I wasn't going to. I began to feel a little sick. But then I reminded myself that this was something I had to do—I had to see my parents. And I would be all right; I'd be able to take care of myself.

Fortunately, before I could think too much more about it there were hugs, kisses, even tears from Aunt Lu, a firm handshake from Uncle Carl. Then Michelle took me through the security check.

Going down the long terminal corridor, I didn't dare look back.

During the takeoff I watched through the window as the St. Louis Arch, the famous Gateway to the West, dropped away below me. Finally it looked small and empty, nothing more than half a McDonald's sign. And then I was going East—to New York City and the Empire State Building!

In New York I was the first passenger off the plane.

"There," said Michelle. "Smooth as anything."

"What about my suitcase?" I asked.

"It's checked right through to London. Nothing to worry about."

I hadn't considered that. It meant I wouldn't be able to change my clothes, or even brush my teeth. But I decided I just wasn't going to worry about that kind of stuff.

Michelle looked at her watch. "We've got plenty of time," she said. "Your flight won't be boarding for an hour. How about a Coke?"

It was time for me to make my move. "I have to go to the bathroom," I told her.

"Sure. Shall I wait for you here?"

"Where's the Coke place?"

"Over there," she said, pointing. "See it? At the far end."

"You can wait for me there," I told her. "Actually, it might take me a while. Don't worry."

"Not sick, are you?" she asked. "You look pale."

"I'm okay," I told her. My heart was pounding. If she could have taken my pulse she probably would have rushed me to an emergency room.

But all she did was say, "I'll wait for you. Now don't get lost, Conrad. I'm responsible for you."

I took off to the men's room, looking back to see if she was watching. She wasn't. Still, just in case, I did go to the men's room, used it, then started to leave. On the way out I stopped, leaned against the wall, and caught my breath, asking myself if I really was going to do what I planned.

Nothing was going to stop me.

Out I went, taking a quick look around. Michelle was nowhere in sight. A crowd of people was heading in the opposite direction from where Michelle would be waiting for me. Quickly, I got right in the middle. Surrounded by tall people I walked down the long ramp. I was halfway home.

At least, that's what I thought.

I had flown to New York City before, but there had always been someone to meet me. This time I was on my own, but I had my next step already planned. It was time to call Nancy Sperling.

I dug the slip of paper with her phone number on it out of my wallet, found a phone booth, dropped in the coins, dialed carefully, and listened as the phone rang with the loud purr of a fat cat.

"Hello?" said a voice.

"Nancy?" I asked, feeling great.

"She isn't here."

She isn't here.

Right then and there, as simple as that—"She isn't here"—my whole plan seemed to crumble. The truth was, I had never even considered that she might not be there.

"Is she going to be there later?" I asked after I got my stomach back.

"Probably."

"Is this her sister?" I tried.

"Who's this?"

"Conrad Murray," I said. "I'm a friend of hers. Do you know when she'll be back?"

"I don't know. She went to a movie. You never know with her. She might get hit by a car."

I couldn't believe what I was hearing, didn't know what to say.

"Do you want her to call you?" the sister said.

"She can't."

"Why not?"

"I'm at the airport."

"Okay. I'll tell her you called."

"Wait!" I managed to get in before she hung up. "Can you tell me where you live?"

"Forty-two Central Park South."

"Okay," I said. Repeating the address over and over, I hung up the phone. Then I frantically wrote the address down on the paper with the phone number.

I stood there, trying to decide what to do. Then all of a sudden I heard a voice booming out over everything: "Would Conrad Murray please report to Pan American Flight Information!"

They were looking for me already. I almost ran out of the terminal. Outside the door were lots of buses, taxis, and cars.

"Want a taxi, kid?" a cab driver yelled at me.

"I have to go to Central Park South," I told him, starting to get into his cab.

"Thirty bucks," he said.

I ducked out fast. Then I tried to remember how far it was to the city, and if I could walk there. The public address system blared again: "Would Conrad Murray please report to Pan American Flight Information!"

A man came by pushing luggage on a wheeled

34

cart. I asked him how to get to the city. "Get on that bus," he advised. "Cheaper than a cab."

I ran to it and climbed on.

We took the highway toward the city, with so many cars around us that I never once saw the road. And when we came up over a rise and the city lay spread out before me, I couldn't believe how big it was. *Huge*. I hadn't remembered it *that* big.

As soon as I got off the bus at the terminal, I found a phone and dialed Nancy Sperling's number again, my heart beating like crazy as I listened to the rings.

The same voice answered.

"Is Nancy there?" I asked hopefully.

"This the person who called before?"

"Yes."

"She called, and I told her what you said. Guess what?"

"What?"

"She said she didn't know anybody by the name of Conrad Murray."

"We're friends. We *are*."

"You still at the airport?"

"I'm at a bus terminal."

"Which one?"

"I don't know."

"You can always try again," said the sister. "Maybe she'll remember who you are." And she hung up.

"See you," I said to the dead phone.

It was already eight o'clock. For a while I wandered around the terminal, trying to make up my mind what to do. Should I wait and call Nancy again or just go to her place? I didn't know; I felt trapped.

I bought a candy bar, then wandered around some more till I came upon some people studying a large city map. A big circle labeled YOU ARE HERE showed me where the terminal was. I found Central Park. It was a big green square. But I couldn't find any Central Park South.

"Excuse me, please," I said to a lady who was looking at the map. "Where's Central Park South?"

She examined me, then moved away as if she thought I was going to attack her or something.

I turned to a guy who was also standing there and asked him. Without looking at me or saying a word, he plumped a fat finger onto a spot right below the green square.

I studied the map for a while, then, making up my mind, I walked out to the street.

There I was, Conrad Murray, age thirteen, in one of the biggest cities in the world, alone, looking for someone I hardly knew.

I mean, I *had* to find Nancy Sperling.

It must have been night somewhere. Not in that city. Not where I was. Not then. The streetlights, glowing blue-white, made the people look like ghosts. And there were so many people, millions of them, rushing, running almost, as if they had to get somewhere before it got too late. The few people who stood in doorways looked like it *was* too late.

After walking west for blocks, I stopped, realizing I didn't know whether I was going the right way. Still, I had to keep moving, and I did, gradually noticing that I was alone. No stores were open. Tall buildings rose up to darkness, except for a few places where there were lights on, little, out-of-reach white boxes. I couldn't see any stars in the sky, only the flashing lights of an airplane. I wondered if it was flying to London and tried to decide if I was sorry not to be on it.

I wasn't sorry. I wasn't going to give up that fast.

I continued to walk until, crossing a wide street, I saw brighter lights and lots of people again, way off to the right. I went in that direction and found myself surrounded by theaters. Now the lights were blinding, banging up against my eyes. I wondered if I would meet my parents going to the shows.

At one corner was a policeman on a horse. The horse, nervous, kept stamping its feet and throwing up its head, while the policeman, in a glistening helmet and silver sunglasses that reflected the neon lights, sat stiff and tall.

"Excuse me, please," I said, going up to him. He didn't hear. "Excuse me, please!" I had to yell.

He looked down and in his glasses I could see myself, an enormous head.

"Where's Central Park South?" I asked.

"Fourteen blocks north," he replied, pointing with his gloved hand. I went the way he showed me.

I'd never seen so many people. Sometimes they moved slowly, sometimes fast, different groups, crisscrossing parades, except there wasn't any music. I let myself be carried along.

At one point the crowd split like water going around a rock. It wasn't a rock; it was a man. He had no legs and he was sitting on a tiny platform with roller-skate wheels. His head was tilted back as if he was looking for something up high. But his eyes couldn't see anything. He was blind. At least the sign around his neck said so: I AM BLIND, it read. There was a painted American flag on it, too, and the words GOD BLESS YOU!!!

There was a cup tied around his neck with a string. Somehow he managed to make his body jump—dancing without any legs—so the few coins in the cup rattled like dice. I don't think I had ever seen anyone work so hard. But nobody gave him a thing.

Then the man, looking as if he was angry but trying not to show it, used what looked like wooden hammers to push himself away. People made way for him, but no one put money in the cup.

When he was gone I was sorry I hadn't given,

sorry I had been so scared. I decided that he probably wasn't blind. All the same, I told myself that if I ever did see him again—and if I had the nerve—I'd give him something. He looked like he needed it.

I continued to walk in the direction the policeman had told me to take. The crowd began to thin, then disappeared. The lights were no longer so bright. I saw that the city had a night, and I didn't like it at all.

Cooing sounds came from above. When I looked up I could make out birds, hundreds of birds sitting on the ledges of buildings whispering to each other. I felt as if they were talking about me.

I walked some more until I found a man closing up his newspaper stand.

"Can you tell me where Central Park South is?"

"Two blocks up," he said, his back to me.

I was tired, but I hurried on, desperate to get there. At the end of two more blocks I had to stop. Across the street was nothing, only a dark green park. I felt like I'd come to the city's edge.

A man and a woman—arms around each other—were standing on the curb waiting to cross. She was wearing a light green blouse and had a sweater tied over her shoulders.

"Can you tell me where Central Park South is?" I asked.

The woman looked down at me with pretty eyes. "You're there," she said softly. Then she and the man crossed the street. For as long as I could I watched the light green of her blouse and thought about her eyes.

Standing there, I looked at what I had written, the number of Nancy's apartment building. Forty-two. Up and down I went, but still I couldn't find the place. The buildings were all tremendous. Sometimes it was even hard to find the numbers. But I found it at last—a door right on the corner. I hadn't even thought to look there.

Number 42 was so huge it took up a whole block. An awning at the entrance reached from door to curb. There was a doorman standing there, tall, fat, with an army-looking cap, a long blue coat that reached his toes, gold braid over one shoulder, red stripes down his arms. *A policeman*, I thought, *from another world.*

I went up to him: "Excuse me, please. I'm looking for Nancy Sperling."

The doorman looked down at me as if I were a mistake. "Miss Sperling?" he said. "Is she expecting you?"

"I told her I was coming, if that's what you mean." He lifted a gloved hand and examined his watch. "She was at the movies," I tried.

A lucky shot. He must have figured I had to be a friend to know where she'd been. His manner changed. "Please step this way, sir. I'll check to see if she's in." Turning around, he held the door open for me.

The foyer we went into was large. It had thick

carpet and a chandelier, and everything was lit up like a year-round Christmas tree.

The doorman went to the desk, picked up the phone, and dialed. "Miss Nancy Sperling, please," he said. "Miss Sperling? There's a young gentleman here to see you." He covered the mouthpiece. "May I have your name, please?"

"Conrad Murray."

"Conrad Murray," he repeated into the phone. As soon as he did I remembered I had given her a different name—Conrad Buckingham—when we'd met in St. Louis.

"She wonders if you can come back tomorrow," said the doorman.

Just hearing that made me feel sick. All I could do was shake my head, no.

"The gentleman says no, miss."

"Tell her I've escaped," I said suddenly. "And tell her my other name is Conrad Buckingham."

The doorman gave me a funny look, but he said it: "The young gentleman—who says his name is also Conrad Buckingham—wishes me to inform you that he's . . . escaped." He looked at me again; then, after listening for a moment; he said, "Yes, miss," and hung up.

I waited.

"She will see you for a few moments," he said.

"Which way do I go?"

"Fourteenth floor," he said, pointing to some elevators. "Apartment E."

I think I ran. In a few minutes I was at Nancy's door.

I was about to knock when the door swung open and there was Nancy Sperling looking out at me. Behind her was an older girl who I guessed must be her sister.

"Hi, Nancy," I said, trying to be as cheerful as I could.

She just stood there and looked at me.

"I . . . ah . . . managed to get away," I said. "You said you could, you know, help."

The two of them simply looked at me.

"Don't you remember?" I said. I felt like I was drowning in the middle of the ocean and had to ask politely for someone to throw me a rope. "You promised to help," I tried.

"He's just a kid," the sister said.

Nancy, saying nothing, just stared at me.

The sister said, "It's kind of late."

"I don't have any other place to go," I said.

Nancy looked at her sister, silently asking her what to do.

"Is anyone with you?" the sister wanted to know.

I shook my head.

"Wait a minute," the sister said. To my horror, they shut the door. That really freaked me out, because I didn't know what I'd do if they didn't let me in. But the next moment the door opened again, wider.

"You can come in for a minute," the sister

said, and they stepped back from the door.

I followed them inside. We went past a small kitchen, then into a large room. It was like nothing I'd ever seen before, I mean, the mess. It's hard to describe. It was everywhere. Clothes lay all over, on the couch, table, chairs, even on the big TV set. There were newspapers, magazines, record albums, records, all just dumped. On the walls were posters, mostly of rock stars. Even they weren't placed right, but were stuck here, there, anyplace, some even falling. There were knives, forks, glasses, dishes. Some had food on them, old food.

After I followed Nancy and her sister into the room, they turned to face me. Nancy looked so different. She was no longer in her school clothes, but in jeans and a baggy sweat shirt. She looked smaller, older.

The sister was bigger than Nancy. I could see that they were sisters, but they didn't look much alike. The sister's face was all made up, with dark around the eyes, and real dark lipstick that glistened. Her hair had been bleached blonde, white blonde, and cut short, like bristles. She had on a tight T-shirt and jeans. Her feet were bare, and her fingernails and toenails were painted a brilliant red. They looked raw. I remembered how I'd thought Nancy was like a zombie. The sister made me think of a vampire.

The two of them sat down on the couch, and Nancy's sister began to study me as if she were a judge and I had done something wrong. As for

Nancy, she looked everywhere but at me. I stood there, feeling I had to say something, only I didn't know what. I just looked around, until finally my eyes landed on that butterfly on Nancy's hand.

I could tell she noticed what I was looking at, because she quickly covered it up with her other hand.

"Do you mind if I use your bathroom?" I asked.

"It's over there," said the sister, pointing.

The bathroom was as much of a wreck as everything else, maybe worse. Makeup junk was spattered all over. On the mirror someone had written in lipstick, FREAK OF THE YEAR!

I looked at myself, surprised at what a mess I was. My face was dirty, my tie was cockeyed and loose, my hair was crazy. I washed up, tried to plaster my hair down. Then I couldn't find a towel. I had to use the sleeve of my jacket.

Back I went to the living room. The two sisters had been talking in low voices. The second I reappeared they stopped.

"What do you mean, you escaped?" Nancy's sister said suddenly. She had dragged one foot up on the couch and was resting her chin on her knee as she examined me.

"Oh, right," I said, feeling myself shift from foot to foot as if I had been brought to the principal's office. I decided I didn't like the sister. But thinking I had no choice, I answered her. "I told Nancy," I said. "My parents, who are rich

44

scientists, live in New York. My aunt and uncle, who take care of me in St. Louis, didn't want me to visit them. So I came on my own. Really, it's true."

"Look, Murray, or Buckingham, or Conrad, or whatever your name is," said the sister, lighting a cigarette, "you seem like an okay kid. But we don't believe you. What's the real story? What do you want from Nancy?"

I was so surprised by that, I couldn't answer. I turned to Nancy to see if I could get any help from her. She gave me nothing. I was beginning to wonder if she even knew how to smile.

"I mean," continued the sister, "you act as if you've been kidnapped or something. That's a lot of crap. Then you told me that your name was Murray, but you told Nancy, here, it was Buckingham. Which is it?"

"Conrad Murray," I said.

I looked at Nancy again, trying to convince myself that she was looking at me in a nice way, but I couldn't be sure if that was true. Sometimes I thought it was, but mostly there was nothing on her face at all.

"Look," said the sister, "we're not going to *do* anything to you for not telling the truth. I happen to lie a lot myself. Big deal. But you're coming to us for help, right? So we have to know. *What is happening?*"

"I never said I was kidnapped," I said. Too upset to make up anything else, I decided to try the truth. "See, my folks, my parents, when they got divorced, they asked my aunt and uncle to be . . . to be my parents."

"When was that?"

"A few years ago."

"This aunt and uncle—don't they like you?"

"Sure they like me."

"Then it's your parents who don't like you," she said.

I shook my head. "That's not true."

"*Somebody* doesn't like you," she insisted.

I could only shake my head again, hating what she was saying, but not able to think how else to answer. I mean, my mind wasn't working normally. If I could have, I would have just left. But there was no other place to go.

"They were sending me to England," I said, not liking the whiny sound in my voice. "We have these cousins there. Only I wanted to come here. So I got off the plane. I couldn't go to my parents right away because that's where everybody will look for me. Besides, they might send me back."

"Maybe nobody will bother to look," said the sister. "Maybe they've been waiting for you to run away. You ever consider that?"

Exhausted, I didn't even answer. I pushed some clothes off a chair and sat.

"What do your parents do?" asked the sister.

"They're actors," I said.

"Really?" she said, showing interest.

I nodded.

46

"Do your aunt and uncle treat you mean?" she continued.

"I told you, no!" I said, worried that I was going to cry. "I just wanted to see my parents!"

"Maybe they don't want to see you," she said.

"That's not true," I whispered, feeling ashamed, even dirty. I didn't want to look at her.

When I finally glanced up, the sisters were looking at each other, but weren't saying anything.

"When did you see your parents last?" asked the sister.

"About a year ago."

"How come you came to this place?" she wanted to know, her voice not so hard.

"I told you," I said. I could feel tears in my eyes. "Nancy is the only other person I know in New York. She said she'd help me."

"And you believed her." The sister shook her head. "You certainly know how to pick winners, don't you? How long do you want to stay?"

"Just tonight. Then I'll call my mom."

Nancy got up and went into the kitchen. I heard the refrigerator door open.

"Did Nancy tell you about our parents?" asked the sister.

"A little," I said.

"They live upstairs," she said. "We live here when we're home from school. I go to college in Vermont."

"This is a nice place," I said, trying to find something to say that would please her.

47

"It's a dump," she snapped back. She said it so sharply that I winced. Then I realized that Nancy had come up behind me with a can of pop and a box of cookies. She didn't say anything, just put them on the table next to me, then went back to sit on the couch. I figured they were for me, so I took a drink and ate.

The sister stood up. "Look, it's all right with me if you stay," she announced. "I don't care." She got up, went into another room, and shut the door behind her.

That left Nancy and me. I took some more cookies and drank some more pop. It made me cold.

"What's her name?" I asked.

"Pat."

"I don't think she likes me."

"She doesn't like anyone."

I didn't know what to make of that, so, to change the subject, I said, "It must be great having your own place. You can do whatever you want."

She didn't say anything for a while. Then she asked, "Doesn't anyone know where you are?"

"Nope. Just you."

"You're all alone."

"Yeah."

"Will your parents be surprised to see you?"

"I guess."

"You could call them now," she said.

"I'll wait till morning," I said, suddenly feeling a little nervous.

"Why?"

I wasn't sure myself. But I said, "I don't want anyone knowing that I'm in New York yet."

"How old are you?" she wanted to know.

"Thirteen," I said, feeling more and more tired. I yawned.

She sat there, not really looking at me, not saying anything. Then she got up and turned on the TV, sat on the floor cross-legged, and started watching a movie.

I kept trying to understand the setup there. I wanted to ask Nancy questions, but I was afraid to. The way they lived seemed crazy. Didn't *feel* right.

"Thanks for letting me stay," I finally said.

She didn't answer, just kept watching TV.

For as long as I could, I watched, too, but my mind wasn't with it. It couldn't have been too long before I fell asleep on the couch, wondering what would happen the next day.

. . .

Saturday Morning

When I woke the next morning the window curtains were open wide, but it was dull outside. I woke slowly, just lying there for a while before I sat up and looked around. It was all so quiet, so different from St. Louis. Back there, I woke up to the sounds of cars, trucks, birds, and Aunt Lu trying to be quiet.

At Nancy's place, I couldn't hear a thing. It might have been a graveyard. I wondered what time it was.

The clock over the kitchen sink said it was almost ten. The box of cookies was still on the table in the living room. So was the empty can. I put the can in the garbage, which was overflowing. Then I took some cookies and ate them.

Suddenly I thought that maybe Nancy and Pat had gone, that they had left me alone. That put me in a panic. I opened one of the bedroom doors and looked in. Nancy was sleeping, sprawled out over her bed, looking more dead than alive.

I felt better right away.

Back in the living room, I took out my wallet and counted my money. I had more than forty bucks. I also took out the paper that Uncle Carl had given me, the one with all the family names, addresses, and phone numbers on it.

I looked around for the phone, but couldn't find it. I was almost glad. I guess I wasn't ready to call yet.

Sitting there, I thought about Aunt Lu and Uncle Carl. I knew that by now they must be very worried, Aunt Lu probably frantic. I felt bad about that. I knew what I had done would be hard on them. I reminded myself that I was doing something I had to do, and that they wouldn't have let me. But I still felt bad. I made up my mind to call them as soon as I had seen my parents.

After taking another handful of cookies, I tried to decide whether I should just leave the apartment or not. I didn't really want to, not until I was sure what would happen when I saw my folks. I needed to know there was a place to come back to.

So I decided to wait. But then it was a question of what to do. I didn't want to turn on the TV. It might have waked the girls. The last thing

I wanted to do was give them an excuse to tell me to leave.

I started to clean up the place. I piled up the newspapers and magazines and put them by the door. I put the records by the stereo. When it came to the clothes, I didn't know what was whose. I just folded everything into one neat pile.

I fixed the wall posters, too, setting them straight. I put the chairs around the table, even emptied the ashtrays. When I found a broom I did some sweeping. I found a carpet sweeper and used that, too. Then I washed the dishes. There was a dishwasher—which was full—but I didn't know how to use it.

I was almost done with the dishes when Nancy came out of her room. It was about eleven-thirty.

She was wearing a pink nightgown and no glasses, and her face was rosy from sleep.

"Hi," I said.

She actually jumped, then scurried back to her room. After a few minutes she came back dressed and with her glasses on.

"Did you have breakfast?" she asked.

"Cookies."

"Want something else? We've got eggs and everything."

"Sure."

I thought she was going to do something about it. Instead, she just sat down at the kitchen table and clasped her hands. It took me a moment to realize she was waiting for me to fix breakfast. I started in.

For a while she didn't say anything. Then, after looking around, she said, "You cleaned up."

"Sure."

"Why?"

I shrugged, not knowing how to answer. I wasn't sure myself. At the same time, I hoped she would say something nice about it. She didn't. She only said, "Did you call your parents?"

"Not yet."

"You can call after breakfast," she said.

I made eggs and toast, even carried the plates to the table. While I was working Nancy waited quietly, not saying another word. I kept wondering what she was thinking, why she didn't talk much. I had never met anyone like her.

When we finished eating she pushed her plate aside. I picked up both our plates, took them to the sink, and started to wash up.

"Why don't you call your parents?" she said.

"I don't know where the phone is."

"We have two," she told me. I watched her go into her room. She brought back a white phone attached to a super-long extension cord. "Mine rings," she said. "Pat's chimes. You don't have to do the dishes. You can call."

I guess I was nervous. Maybe I was even afraid to call. So I finished washing the dishes first. I could tell Nancy was anxious for me to call. I figured she wanted me out of the place.

When I was finally ready, I pulled out my sheet of phone numbers and unfolded it. Just when I was about to reach for the phone, it rang. It made us both jump. Automatically I picked the phone up and said, "Hello?"

For the longest time the person on the other end didn't say anything. Then a woman's voice said, "Who is this?"

"Conrad," I said.

After another pause the voice said, "This is Nancy's mother. May I speak to her?"

I handed the phone to Nancy. "Your mother," I said.

"Hello," said Nancy cautiously. "A friend of mine. We're in the kitchen. He's . . . twelve. He's visiting with his parents . . . No. Just came. . . . From St. Louis. . . . I have a lot of schoolwork to do today. . . . Tomorrow for dinner. I hadn't forgotten. . . . I'll tell her. 'Bye."

Then she gave the phone back to me. I hung up, expecting her to say something. She didn't.

"Does she mind that I'm here?" I asked.

Nancy shrugged.

I stared at her. But she just wasn't going to give.

"Are you going to call your parents?" she said.

"I guess," I said. I dialed my mother's number slowly, carefully, while Nancy waited, hands clasped.

The phone rang three times. "Hi!" came a bright voice.

"Mom!" I shouted, suddenly excited.

"This is Denise Murray on a recorded message," my mom's voice went on to say. "I'm very busy right now. Just let me know who's calling and I'll get back to you if you leave your number. You can speak for as long as you like. 'Bye!" Then there was a beep, and the phone seemed to go dead.

I put the phone down. I felt as if I had been all ready for a race, the gun had gone off, and I had started—only to hit a brick wall that was right in front of the starting line.

"Not there?" asked Nancy.

"A message," I got out. "She said I could leave one."

"An answering machine," said Nancy. "Did she say when she's coming back?" She was watching me very closely.

I was so upset I could only shake my head. In fact it took me a while to find my voice again. "Maybe," I said, "maybe I should just go there and surprise her."

"Where does she live?" asked Nancy.

I read from the paper. "One thirty-nine Remsen Street. Brooklyn. Do you know where that is?"

She shook her head.

Her eyes on me were making me feel I had to say more, so I gave her the big actor bit. "She's an important actress," I said. "Maybe she's off making a movie, or something for TV. I see her on TV lots of times," I lied.

When Nancy didn't say anything, I stood up.

"I guess I should go," I said. "I'll wait for her there." But I was still feeling shaky, and didn't really want to go at all.

"What about your father?" asked Nancy.

"Oh, yeah," I said. After checking the paper, I dialed. The phone rang about thirty times before I put it down. "Not there," I told her. "He lives on Tiemann Place. Know where that is?"

She shook her head.

"Maybe they're in a play together," I said. "They used to do things like that. Or—he's in charge of Macy's department store. He could be there."

"It's all right to wait here," she said.

"What about Pat?"

"Don't pay attention to her. She likes to say things to upset people," Nancy said. "I was planning to go to a movie. If you'd like, you could come with me."

"I thought you said you had schoolwork."

She didn't say anything, so I said, "Okay," glad not to have to be on my own.

"I'll get my things," she said. She gathered up her phone and started to take it back to her room. But halfway there she stopped. "Conrad," she said, "you don't have to make up things about your parents. I don't care what they are."

For the first time I felt like she was really talking to *me*. I didn't know which I was more, embarrassed or relieved. Anyway, there was nothing I could say.

. . .

Saturday Afternoon

It was still gray outside when we left. The grayness seemed to be everywhere: gray buildings, gray sidewalks, gray people. And in the daylight I could see how filthy all the streets were, as if the neighborhood dogs had knocked over every garbage can in town.

All those people were back again. I tried to look at them all. They reminded me of the huge jigsaw puzzles my Aunt Lu was always working on—the five-thousand-piece size. Aunt Lu complained that all the pieces seemed to be the same. In New York City the people-pieces were all different.

Nancy wasn't looking at the people. She just stared in front of her, looking at things that only she could see. I was reminded of that first time I'd seen her, when she hadn't seemed connected to anything or anybody. She walked fast. I had to work hard to keep up.

"Where're we going?" I finally asked.

"Central Cinema I."

"You went to the movies last night," I said. "You go a lot, don't you?"

She said nothing.

"Do you like movies that much?"

She didn't answer that either, just kept walking.

I tried to figure out why she didn't answer some questions. In the end I decided that she didn't answer when she didn't like what I was getting at, and that maybe it was better not to ask too much. Still, I kept trying to guess what she was thinking. I couldn't. She was too good at not letting me know.

"Why did you talk to me that day in St. Louis, at the travel agent's?" she asked suddenly. It had to be the last thing I expected her to say.

"I don't know," I admitted. "I just did." But when I thought about it, I remembered that she had talked to me first. I decided not to remind her of that.

"Was it the way I looked?" she wanted to know. "Or was it something I was doing?"

"I told you," I said, taking an extra step to keep up. "I don't know. Lucky, I guess."

She shot a look at me and I thought she would say something, but she didn't. She was as serious as ever. It gave me an idea.

"You ever laugh?" I asked.

She didn't reply, just kept her eyes straight forward. They could have made rulers out of her looks.

"I mean, how come you're so serious all the time?" I wanted to know. "Don't you like funny things?"

She wouldn't answer. She just started walking even faster.

"I have a reputation for being able to get people to laugh," I told her. "Want me to get you to laugh?"

"We're almost to the movie," she said.

"Bet I could get you to laugh," I said. When she didn't say anything I jumped in front of her, swung around, and started to walk backward, facing her.

She didn't like it, and stopped.

"Just trying to get you to laugh," I said.

"I'm perfectly fine," she said, and she started to walk again.

The way she was acting only made me want to try even harder to get her to laugh. We continued side by side until we got near a couple on the sidewalk, talking. I ran up to them. "Excuse me, please," I said in a voice loud enough for Nancy to hear. "My friend is a princess from the kingdom of Zwang. Can you speak Zwangle?"

"I'm sorry," said the man politely. "I can't. Perhaps the public library can help you."

Nancy swept past and I had to run to catch up.

"Please don't do that," she said. But watching her, I thought she almost smiled.

Then, a little farther down the block, I noticed a small grocery store. A man was setting out boxes of fruit. I went over to him. "Excuse me, please," I said. "Do you have any fresh frobish?"

"What?" said the man.

"Frobish," I said, trying to keep from laughing. "But it has to be fresh." Nancy stopped, keeping her distance, but watching.

"Hey, Barney!" the groceryman called to someone inside. "We got any frobish? Fresh?"

"Naw," came a voice. "Not today. Monday, for sure."

"Okay, thank you," I said. We walked on, and I knew Nancy was really trying to keep herself from smiling, maybe even from laughing. I was making progress. I figured if I could do one more thing like that—something good—I could make her laugh.

All of a sudden Nancy stopped. "They've changed the movie," she said.

"So what?" I said. I hadn't even noticed we'd reached the theater.

"It's R-rated."

Right away I got my idea and went up to the ticket seller. "Two adult, please," I said, taking out my wallet.

The ticket woman, who had been reading a newspaper, looked up, first at me, then at Nancy. "This is an R-rated movie," she said. "How old are you?"

Before Nancy could say anything, I said, "Don't worry. We're older than we look. She's my wife. How much is it?"

The ticket seller hesitated for a moment, staring at us, but when she saw my money, she took it and gave me two adult tickets. Expensive.

As we moved up to the ticket taker, I saw Nancy grin.

It was worth it.

The movie was dumb. It was supposed to be a love story, but I wasn't even sure it was. Everything was in some foreign language, Italian I think, so I couldn't really understand what was happening. There were subtitles, but I hate reading movies.

Nancy liked it, though. She just sat there, watching closely. I watched her more than I watched the movie.

"Could you understand that?" I asked when we got out.

She nodded.

"Did you like it?"

She nodded again.

"Why?"

She wouldn't answer. Instead, she looked at her wristwatch, then said, "Why don't you try calling your parents again?"

It didn't work out so easily. First we had to find a phone that worked. We kept walking, but every phone we came to was out of order. Finally we found one that was okay. I stepped inside the booth, leaving the door open so Nancy could hear.

At my mother's, I got the recorded message again. At my father's, all I got was rings. I gave up.

"How about something to eat?" I suggested. I was starving.

She said, "Okay," then took me to a restaurant right around the corner. It was a fancy place where you had to go upstairs, and it had this very quiet feeling. The waiters were all dressed up. One of them seemed to know Nancy. After bowing, he took us to a table, even held the chair for Nancy. I was glad I had my tie on. I slipped the knot up.

Then the waiter presented us with these gigantic menus. When I looked at the prices I nearly died. As soon as the waiter bowed off, I whispered, "This is a mistake!"

"Why?"

"Too expensive!"

"Doesn't matter."

"Well, you eat, then. I don't have that kind of money."

She said, "I'll pay for this. You paid for the movie."

"That was because you were my wife."

She put her menu down. "Why did you say that?"

"Trying to get you to laugh."

She looked down in front of her and didn't say anything.

I tried to kid her. "You mean you already want to get divorced?"

The waiter sneaked up from nowhere, reminding me of Count Dracula. "Would you care to order?" he said.

"Ask my wife what she wants first," I said.

Even as Nancy turned red, the guy did a double take. He turned to her in surprise. "Really married, Miss Sperling?" he said.

Nancy shook her head violently.

"Don't let her fool you," I said. "We're on our honeymoon."

The waiter was smiling as he went away. But I could see that Nancy was really unhappy about what I had said. I was beginning to think the gag was a mistake.

Then the waiter came back with two wine-glasses and a bottle all wrapped up in a towel.

"Compliments of the house," he said with a bow, and poured a little of the stuff into the glasses.

"What is it?" I wanted to know.

"Ginger ale, sir," said the waiter. "And a very good year. Our felicitations on your marriage."

I thought it was funny. But when Nancy still didn't say anything, I decided to shut up before she got mad. I searched the menu for a hamburger.

By the time we were finished eating I had made up my mind that it was time to try calling my parents again. Nancy must have been thinking the same thing, because the minute we left the place she said, "Aren't you going to call again?"

That made me think that she was trying to find a way to get rid of me. "You don't have to stay with me," I said.

"What if you don't find them?"

"I will."

She said nothing, and neither did I, because I didn't really want her to leave me. Then I tried calling again, but no one was there at either place. Afterward we stood on the sidewalk, not sure what to do next. It was getting to be late afternoon.

"If I knew where my mother's place was, I'd just go wait there," I said. "Then you wouldn't have to worry."

"We can take a taxi," she said. "They always know." Before I could say anything she had hailed a cab.

The driver asked where we were going.

"One thirty-nine Remsen Street, Brooklyn."

"Brooklyn! Oh, Jesus, kids," the driver complained. "I don't know Brooklyn. Take the subway. This'll cost you a fortune."

I started to get out, but Nancy said, "We can pay."

Grunting, the driver started his meter, then consulted a little book. "Brooklyn Heights," he announced. "Not so bad," and we started.

Though it seemed as if we had to drive through the whole city, it didn't take so very long. We passed the Empire State Building, and a while after that we drove over the Brooklyn Bridge. Right after the bridge we went into a section with a lot of small houses and trees. Pretty soon the cab driver said, "Here's your place."

We got out, and Nancy paid.

It was a quiet, narrow street. The trees weren't big, and they didn't look very healthy. Their bark was paper thin, their new leaves already brittle. Some of the leaves had even turned brown. The houses were all brown too. And the sidewalks weren't smooth; they were made of big square slabs of blue-gray stone, no two stones alike or level with each other.

We stood on the sidewalk for a while, looking at 139 Remsen Street. Like the other houses, it had five stories.

I opened the front door and we stepped into a little entryway with a whole row of mailboxes. It was a small house, but a lot of people seemed to live there. I saw my mother's box right away. Through a little window I could see that there was mail inside. Under the box was a white button. I pushed it; nothing happened.

"Not there," said Nancy.

"Maybe she's in Hollywood," I began. Nancy looked around quickly. "Or somewhere," I added, feeling that she could tell right away when I wasn't telling the truth.

"We can wait," she suggested.

Which is what we did. We went out front and

leaned against one of the parked cars.

"Why did you decide to come like this?" she asked. That was her way, asking hard questions right out of the blue.

"I wasn't sure what was happening with my parents," I said, hoping she wouldn't ask any more.

"How come you've never been to this place before?" she asked.

"We used to live in the suburbs before my folks split up. When I went to St. Louis, they moved in to Manhattan. To a few different places. My mother hasn't lived here very long."

While we were waiting there the door of the building opened and a man leading a dog on a leash came out. We watched them as they went down the street.

"I wonder if he knows where she is," I said. I decided to ask him when he came back. In the meantime, for no reason, I went back in and tried the buzzer a few times. Nothing happened.

The man and his dog were gone a long time, and when the man came back he was halfway through the door before I got up the nerve to speak to him.

"Excuse me, please," I said. "I'm looking for Denise Murray. Do you know where she is?"

The man looked me up and down, then at Nancy. The dog sniffed at my shoes. "Denise?" he said. "You can try her buzzer."

"It doesn't answer."

"She's in and out a lot," he said. "She expecting you?"

"Not really. I'm her son."

He looked at me with new interest. "So you're Conrad. I thought you lived out in the Midwest or something. You do look like her a little. Not home, huh?"

"Do you know when she'll be back?" I asked.

"Can't say that I do," he said. "How come you're here?"

"Visiting."

He considered this for a moment. Then he said, "I'm Bob Appleton. My place is the apartment right over hers. I have to go out later, but if you'd like, you can wait there for a while. You'd hear if she came in."

"Sure, thanks," I said, and we followed him and his dog in. The dog was all excited.

Bob Appleton led the way up. At the third floor he stopped. "That's her apartment at the end," he said.

I took a look at the door; then we went up another flight.

He unlocked his apartment with three different keys. Once we were inside he locked the door behind us, even putting an iron wedge against it.

It was a tiny place, two small rooms and a very small bathroom. Each room had a window, but they all had bars on them. One window looked out at another window, another down onto someone's rubbish heap, and the bathroom window was frosted so you couldn't look out. The place was like a jail cell. I wondered how anyone could live there all cooped up. I hoped my mom's place was better.

"She did know you were coming, didn't she?" Bob Appleton asked me.

"Not exactly," I fudged.

He gave me a funny look.

There wasn't much to do but sit and wait. The dog played with us for a while, then went to sleep. Bob Appleton went into the other room to do some kind of work.

As we sat there, I began to imagine that something was wrong downstairs, that my mother was in there sick or something. Once I got this idea into my head, even though I knew it was probably stupid, it just kept coming back. Finally I jumped up and went to the doorway of the other room and asked Bob what he thought.

"I'm sure she isn't sick," he said. "I saw her a couple of days ago. She was fine then. I would have known."

"Are you a good friend of hers?"

"Yeah, I guess so."

"Maybe if I went down there and knocked on the door . . ." I said, still not satisfied, "Maybe the buzzer isn't working. . . . "

He got up. "If it's really bothering you, we'd better check," he said. "I have a key to her apartment." When I didn't say anything, he seemed to feel he had to explain. "She gave it to me in case she ever lost hers. She's always losing stuff. Come on. It'll make you feel better."

We went downstairs and he unlocked my mom's door. The apartment was just like his, small, really cramped. Though I had never been there before, it seemed familiar, even the smell—but I stopped noticing that after a second.

It wasn't very neat—not messy the way Nancy's and Pat's place was, but crowded with things. The bed wasn't made, there were stockings on the floor, a dress thrown over a chair, shoes and slippers all over. It made me think how funny it was that my mom and Aunt Lu were sisters. On the desk where the phone was, next to the answering machine, there were lots of scribbled notes, lists of things to do.

On a little dresser was a picture of me when I was eight, in a Little League suit. I wondered why she didn't have one that showed me older; I always sent her my latest school picture.

We were just standing there when the phone rang. It made everybody jump. We all took a step toward it, then just stopped and waited. It rang three times. Then, out of the speaker in the answering machine came my mother's voice.

"Hi! This is Denise Murray on a recorded message. I'm very busy right now. Just let me know who's calling and I'll get back to you if you leave your number. You can speak for as long as you like. 'Bye!"

Then came the beep, and, right away, another voice: Aunt Lu's.

69

"This is Lu *again*, Denise. How many messages can I leave? It's past five o'clock your time and I'm simply insane with worry about Conrad. I've heard absolutely nothing! If he's reached you, for heaven's sake, please, *please* call me. None of your nonsense, Denise, please. I've tried to reach that fool who was your husband, but God knows where he is. And Denise, honey, I'm warning you, if this is just another one of your idiotic, immature stunts, I'll come up there just to slap your face. Didn't I *plead* with you to take him? Only for a week, Denise. He really wanted to see you. It was *you* who said no. I know how you're struggling, but . . . I'm truly beside myself. . . . I can't even think right. Now, *please*, Denise, when you come back, *if* by the grace of the good Lord you ever *do* come back, call me instantly. We have to find that boy!"

I stood there, stunned, not really believing what I had heard—that the whole England trip thing was a lie, that the reason Aunt Lu and Uncle Carl hadn't sent me to New York was that my mother hadn't wanted me to come. And it wasn't just what Aunt Lu had said. It was the way she had said it. I mean, I don't think I had ever seen her angry, at *anybody*. But there she was, angry at my mother, and it was my fault. I didn't know what to do.

Bob Appleton and Nancy kept looking at me, waiting for me to say something. I just couldn't. No way.

It was Bob who spoke first. "What in God's name is going on?" He was really upset.

"Nothing," I managed to say.

"Where are you supposed to be?" he demanded. "Did you run away from someplace?"

"No."

"Who was that woman?"

"I don't know."

"What's she to you?"

"Never heard of her before."

"Don't you think you'd better tell her where you are?"

"No reason to," I said.

"You can use that phone," he said. "You can even use *my* phone if you want to."

I kept standing there.

"Now listen, kids," said Bob, looking at his watch. "I have to go out. I feel a little funny about letting you stay here. To tell the truth, I don't think you should. But if you want to, you can stay up in my place. Conrad, how about *my* calling that woman? What's her number?"

I eyed Nancy. She gave me no answers.

"We have to go back to Nancy's house," I said.

"Then give me your number there. Nancy, what's your parents' name?"

"She doesn't live with her parents," I said.

"Now, *listen*," said Bob, getting more and more upset, "I am *trying* to be helpful. But you have to cut out the nonsense. What the hell is going on?"

Nancy had moved to the door and was waiting by it. I began to edge toward her. "I'll call later," I said. "Thanks for the help."

"Kids," he said, "I really think you're making a mistake. Look, forget about my going out. I'll stay with you. I'll—"

I didn't hear the rest. Nancy and I ran down the stairs and out of the building. We raced down the street, running as if someone was chasing us. We turned a corner, kept on going. Only at the next block did we stop to catch our breath.

We stood there, panting.

I felt I had to say something. "I never heard my aunt talk that way before," I said. "She's upset. I mean, I guess I should have called." As always, I was feeling that I was supposed to take care of my aunt and uncle. That when I didn't, things just came apart.

Nancy stood there, breathing heavily, looking at me in that way she had.

I guess it was then that I realized something about her. There I was trying to figure her out, while she was doing the same to me. I had this feeling that she was trying to look into me, trying to see the way I worked, testing me. Sure enough, she said, "Why don't you call, then? Tell your aunt where you are."

Her saying that reminded me that what I was doing was for me, not for them. I wasn't going to take care of them anymore. "No," I told her. "I don't want to." And I started to walk, not in any particular direction, just to move. She followed.

...

Saturday Evening

It was getting dark.

"Maybe we should go back to my place," Nancy said.

I didn't answer her. I just took out my phone number list again, deciding that I had to show her I wasn't afraid. "My father might be home now," I said.

We walked some more, looking for a phone booth. Nancy spotted one first. As soon as I saw it, I had second thoughts. I guess my Aunt Lu's anger was on my mind. Maybe my father would be angry, too. But I felt I had to call—I couldn't put it off anymore.

I dropped in my dime and dialed while Nancy stood nearby. The phone began to ring. I expected it to ring forever. Maybe I wanted it to. This time someone answered.

"Hello?" came a voice. It was my father.

"Hello?" he said again. "Who is this? Darn! Do you want to talk or not?"

I hung up the phone. "He's there," I announced.

"Why didn't you say anything?"

I wasn't sure myself. "I think I should just go there," I said, my heart beating fast.

"He might leave," she warned. "I think you should tell him you're coming."

"I'd rather just go," I said.

Once again we took a taxi through the city.

Tiemann Place was a very wide street, on a hill, with cobblestones instead of pavement, and at the bottom of the hill an elevated train track. On both sides of the street were enormous apartment buildings.

This time I paid the fare—a lot—and we found ourselves standing outside one of the buildings.

"Do you want to go alone?" Nancy asked.

I shook my head. We went inside, into a long, wide area full of heavy glass doors and black ironwork. There were lots of mailboxes, some of them broken. It took me a while to find my father's. But finally I found it—Number 704—and pushed the button under it.

"Hello?" came a loud, ragged voice. "Is that someone coming? Darn! Who is it? . . . Why aren't you answering?"

It sounded like my father, but at the same time, it didn't. Before I could make up my mind what to say, there was a loud buzzing sound. Nancy pushed up against one of the glass doors, and it opened.

"Are you really sure you want me to go?" she asked when we reached the elevators. "I could wait here."

"I want you to meet him," I said. "Don't you want to?"

"I thought you might rather see him alone."

A thought came to me. "You're scared of what might happen, aren't you?"

She wouldn't say what she was thinking.

"Come on," I said, as if I wasn't scared myself.

We took the elevator to the seventh floor, stepped out, and faced twenty doors. They were identical except for the numbers. I rang the bell next to 704.

The door was opened a crack. At first all I could see was his eyes—small, wet, careful.

"Hi, Dad," I said.

The door opened the rest of the way. My father stared at me. I guess he didn't understand at first who I was.

"It's me," I said. "Conrad. Your kid."

My father's clothes never did seem to fit. His pants were always too long, the white shirts he wore—with the cuffs turned back and the top button open so you could see his undershirt—always all baggy. His face wasn't so much long as droopy. And he had round glasses and sandy, graying hair that fell over his forehead.

75

He kept his arms up, elbows close to his body. He reminded me of a boxer who was defending himself and not doing a very good job of it. "Conrad?" he said. It was a question. I guess he didn't really believe it was me.

I grinned. Inside, I was very nervous.

"Conrad," he repeated, his voice not altogether there. It took a moment for the thing to sink deep. Then he exploded. "Conrad! Well, my God, my *God*! Holy smokes. Darn! You didn't tell me. I was just getting ready to go out. . . . My God! Conrad! Don't just stand there. Come on in. My God . . . I was just—" He saw Nancy. "Hi," he said. "I didn't see you."

"She's my friend," I said.

"Well, sure, sure. A friend. That's what friends are for. Visit your dad right out of the blue. Good God! Come on in!" He was so excited he seemed to fold himself in fifteen directions at once—origami style—and each new side had to say the same things.

His place had a long hallway that led to three rooms at the far end. He all but pushed us back there, into the living room.

It was packed with furniture: a table, two small couches, chairs, a sideboard, a TV. The TV was on. Opposite it was a huge tilt-back chair, and a small table next to that. On the small table was an open can of beer.

"I was just getting ready to go out," he repeated. "Heavy date. Just got back from work and the phone rang. Was that you? Then the door buzzer from downstairs rang. You, too? Conrad, why didn't you tell me? My God, amazing! Here, let me look at you." He touched me on the shoulder with a finger, then stepped back and eyed me up and down.

"You're looking good," he said. "You are. By God, you've gotten big. Hasn't he?" he said to Nancy. "But what are you doing here? How come you didn't tell me you were coming? Is something wrong? How's your Aunt Lu and Uncle Carl? Does your mother know you're here? Of course she does. You'd tell her. Smart woman. Too smart for me. By God!"

I wanted to answer his questions, but there were too many of them. Besides, he didn't give me any time. I turned to look at Nancy, but she had retreated into a chair in the corner, doing her zombie act. I felt embarrassed, like it was all a mistake, like I wanted to start all over again and get it right.

"You need something to eat?" he pushed on. "I don't know what I have. But we can find something. Sardines! You were always big on sardines. By God, Conrad, what are you doing here?"

"I just thought I'd visit," I said.

"Great! Perfectly great. Darn! You're about two inches taller than the last time I saw you, you know. Bet you're stronger than me, too. When did I see you last?"

"About a year ago."

"Right. We didn't have much time, did we? I

77

mean, things didn't work out. And, darn, I know I don't write enough. You don't have to tell me. You did get my Christmas present though, didn't you?"

He wasn't acting the way I wanted him to act, calm, talking easy, relaxed. My visit was really upsetting him.

"Sure, I got it," I said.

"A model, right? Spaceship. Starship *Enterprise*. Best thing in the whole store. Most expensive, too, you know. See, I don't forget. I thought you'd go for it. Nothing's too good for you. By God, don't just stand there. This is your house, too!"

With a sudden jump he ran over to the TV set and turned it off.

"Go on, sit," he urged.

I sat, not knowing what else to do. I felt like shutting my eyes, not even looking at him. He was fluttering all over the place, almost dancing, fussing with his cuffs, sliding the knot of his necktie up and down, rubbing his hair, nervous as anything.

"Now," he finally said, taking a seat opposite me, "tell me everything. I mean, what's *really* happening? My God!"

"I told you. I just came. That's all."

"Just like that?" He turned to Nancy. "Is he telling the truth? Your Aunt Lu let you?" he said back to me. "Guess I don't give her enough credit. I always thought—you know—she didn't like me. Not that I ever heard her say so. She

78

wouldn't say it, not in public. How long're you going to stay?"

"I don't know," I said.

"Hey," he said, "*is* something wrong? Is everything okay out there? Something the old man can do for you?"

"Nope."

"Just wanted to see me, right?" He turned to Nancy again. "Is that for real?" he asked her. "Are you from St. Louis, too?"

"Yes, sir," she said, using the same voice I had heard when I'd first met her.

"*Sir*? By God, you couldn't say that and be from New York. I've had a long day," he said, leaping up and then flinging himself into his big tilt-back chair. "Let me tell you, a *long* one. The economy is soft now. Everything is slack. You really have to push to make people buy." He swiveled up and leaned forward, jabbing the air as he talked, almost shadowboxing. "They want to buy, but you see, they're afraid to, to spend all that money."

He jumped up and began to act. " 'Madam,' I say, 'let me assure you, just between you and me, the price of this chair is going up on Monday. My floor manager just gave me the word. Up twenty percent!' You have to whisper that," he said. "Good effect. 'Really?' she says. You have to sound good here. 'Cross my heart and hope to die,' I say. They always shake their heads. Then I say, 'It breaks my heart. People won't be able to afford any quality after a while,

79

not like this.' And then I say, 'Pretty soon'—this is the clincher—'pretty soon people will only be able to buy junk. And I hate to sell junk.'

"Mind you," he went on, "it's *all* junk. But that's life, right? Furniture is a strange thing. People live with it forever. That couch you're sitting on, Conrad, remember it? We had it when we lived out on Long Island. There's a spot where you dumped ketchup on it, or something. I don't remember. Your mother never liked that couch. But it's one of the few good things I got out of that marriage. Wouldn't part with it for the world."

He looked at me bleakly.

I suppose he wanted me to say something. I couldn't. I didn't know what he was talking about. It sounded like a lot of gibberish. I looked at Nancy. She was staring at my father.

"Have you seen your mother?" he said.

I shook my head.

"Why not?" he snapped. "She'd be upset if you didn't. You know that, don't you? Darn!" he said. Then his mood changed again. "Conrad, I want you to know, I still love your mother. By God, I'd like to get us all together again, but . . . By God, it's great to see you!

"Oh, Lord," he said suddenly, looking at his watch. "I'm supposed to meet someone!" He dashed into another room and I heard him dial the phone. "No answer," he said, coming back. "She'll be waiting." But he didn't explain.

Trying to find something to talk about, I asked, "How's your acting?"

He looked around, surprised. "Acting? Hard, real hard. You know, to be a good actor, you need energy. *Energy!* A great Russian theater director, I think it was him. . . . It's in a book . . ." He looked around. "Where *is* that book? Anyway," he said, giving up the search, "an actor must have energy to burn! God, he was right. To *burn*. But, see, I use my energy up in the store, selling. I mean, it's a kind of acting, right? On a set. Audience of one. See, I just don't have time to act. Oh, I go to the theater. Well, once in a while. Darned expensive. I don't have that kind of money. But no, mostly, not enough time. Still, you never know. I mean, after all, by God, you're here." He collapsed into a chair. "Things do turn out funny, don't you think?"

"I guess," I said.

"Hey," he said, leaning forward with a quick glance at his watch. "Where you staying?"

"Nancy's place."

He looked at her again. "I thought you were from St. Louis." He jumped up with his arms out and began to sing and strut.

> *"Meet me in St. Louis, Louis,*
> *Meet me at the fair,*
> *Don't tell me the lights are shining*
> *Any place but there,*
> *We will dance the Hoochee Koochee . . .*

"You ever see that movie?" he asked Nancy. "Judy Garland! *Great* movie. Ever see it?"

"No, sir."

"How about that?" He stared at her, then turned back to me. "Conrad, how's school? Doing all right? Getting good grades? Conrad's smart, clever," he said to Nancy. "Knew it from the start. I used to tell his mother that. Gets it from her. You *are* going to see her, aren't you?"

"Sure."

"Conrad," he said, lowering his voice confidentially. "You in some kind of trouble?" He took a quick look at Nancy, then turned right back to me.

The question made me angry, and I didn't answer. I had told him why I'd come, but it was as if he couldn't understand the reason, didn't want to.

"Are you?" he asked, his voice rising. "I mean, can I help you with anything? You just have to ask, right? You know that. You don't have to hold back. You can be open with me. I'm your father. Anything!"

"I'm not in any trouble," I said.

"And you really came just to see me?" he said, with another fast glance at his watch.

"Yes," I said.

"How come?" he demanded, becoming angry. "There *has* to be more in it than that. By God, there *has* to be. I want the truth now, boy!"

"It *is* the truth," I said, not understanding why

he wouldn't accept what I was saying.

"Do your Uncle Carl and Aunt Lu know where you are?"

"No," I said.

"*My God*," he whispered. And he sank into his chair again.

For a time nobody said anything. My father just sat there, shaking his head, looking at me, sometimes at Nancy, sometimes snatching what he thought were secret glances at his watch. At last he sprang to his feet. "Let's you and me talk a minute, okay?" he said, nodding toward the door.

"That's all right," I said. "I don't keep any secrets from Nancy." The truth was, it was hard enough with her there. Alone with him it would have been a lot worse.

He stared at me hard. "Okay," he said. "I didn't know you were coming. Someone is waiting for me. I can't reach her. . . . Darn! Look, I want to know what's going on, Conrad. Something is wrong. I know it. I have a right to know. By God, I'm your father. You come here out of the blue, you bring your friend. You say your Aunt Lu doesn't know where you are. And you haven't seen your mother. *I want to know what's going on!*" he shouted.

"I told you," I said. "I wanted to see you. That's all there is to it."

He still refused to accept it. "Are they treating you badly? Doing something they shouldn't?

They promised to keep me informed. Well, they don't. But . . . *what* is going on?"

I couldn't say it again. I couldn't.

"Conrad, there's a phone in there. Don't you think you should call your aunt and tell her where you are? You don't have to tell her you're with me. She wouldn't like that. Believe me, I'd catch a lot of hell. . . . But . . . well, tell her you're with your friend here. What did you say her name was?"

"Nancy Sperling."

He closed his eyes. "Conrad, when do you intend to go back?"

"After I see Mom."

"Well, go call her then."

"She's not there."

He jumped up, rushed into the other room and dialed. In moments I heard him speak very fast, so fast I knew he was leaving a message: "Denise? This is Noel. *Disaster!* Conrad has shown up. Here, in New York, my place. I can't make out his story. I don't know why he's come and I don't know what to do. Please call as soon as you get in. But I have to go out. Thanks. *Please*, Denise, *answer this call!*"

He came back, checking his wallet. "Look," he said after a moment. "I have to go." He snapped his fingers. "Darn! Come with me. Double date! What do you say, kids?"

I stood up. He wanted to go, and I wasn't going to ask him not to. "We have to leave," I said.

"No, really," he said. "Why don't you come?

Or look, stay here. I'll bring my friend back."

"We have to go somewhere," I said. Nancy got up, too.

"What about tomorrow?" he said. "No, darn," he checked himself. "Can't. I know, Monday. Meet me for lunch, Conrad. Come to the furniture department at about . . . one-thirty. Take you to lunch. Staff room. Meet the boys. Hey, the Empire State Building. I promised, didn't I? See, I do remember. I keep my promises. How about that?"

"Okay," I said, just wanting to leave.

"Great," he said. "We'll live it up. Get it? Up? Top of the Empire State Building. You're not going to forget, are you?"

He walked us to the door, opened it. "Monday, one-thirty, Conrad. Lunch. My treat. Meet me in St. Louis, Louis, just the two of us. Though you can come too, Nancy Sperling. Conrad, man to man!"

As Nancy went out into the hall, my father partially closed the door behind her, keeping me in. "Conrad," he said, his voice lowered. "You know I . . . I love you, right?"

"Sure," I said.

"You just caught me by surprise. I can't even give you any money. And someone's waiting for me. Hey, you'd like her. Great sense of humor. And you love me, too, right? It's corny, but you do, right?"

I looked up at him.

"Come on, kid, don't be embarrassed. Say you love the old man. I need that, too."

"Sure," I said.

He took my hand and began to pump it up and down. "My God! Monday at one-thirty. Be on time. I only get forty-five minutes."

I stepped out into the hall. Nancy was holding the elevator door open.

"One-thirty, old man!" my father called. "We'll live it up!"

We got into the elevator; the doors shot shut. Nancy pressed the button and we started down. I didn't dare look at her.

When we got outside the streetlights were on. A whole swarm of bugs were fluttering madly around one of them. At the bottom of the hill, at the elevated station, a train rumbled in, stopped, then went off again.

I didn't know what to say, to feel, to think. For the first time I wished Nancy wasn't there. I didn't even want to look at her. I was so afraid of what she might say. Then she lifted her hand and touched my face. It was the hand with the butterfly.

"Want to go to a movie?" she said.

. . .

Saturday Night

I didn't watch the movie. It might have been in color or black-and-white, in English or Chinese. I don't know. I might even have slept through it all. I honestly don't remember.

Nancy did watch it. When I asked her afterward if she liked it, she said it wasn't bad.

"How many movies do you go to when you're in New York?" I asked as we headed back to her apartment.

"It depends on how long I'm staying."

"One a day?"

"Sometimes."

"More?"

"Sometimes."

"Do your parents know?"

"No."

"Do you ever go to the movies in St. Louis?"

"No."

"Why not?"

"I like it there."

"What about studying? You get good grades?"

"Yes."

"What did you think of me when I showed up at your school that time?"

"You frightened me."

"How come?"

"You knew what I wanted to do."

"I did?"

She nodded, yes.

"How did that happen?"

"That's what I'm trying to figure out," she said.

When we reached the apartment, Pat was there with some guy. They were playing cards. The guy looked up when we came in, said "Hello," but kept on playing. Pat didn't say anything.

Nancy and I went into the kitchen. This time she helped find stuff and put it together. We made peanut butter sandwiches.

"Who's the guy?" I asked.

"I don't know."

Though I ate a lot, Nancy hardly ate anything.

"What's the matter?" I said.

"I'm not hungry," she said. "Are you going to call your mother again?"

"I guess so."

"What about your aunt and uncle?"

I considered it.

"You should."

"Why?"

"Your father will get into trouble," she said. Without saying anything else she went and brought back her phone.

"How come you're so worried about *him*?" I wanted to know. "What about me? Don't you care how I feel?"

"Is that what you think?" she said.

"You never answer straight," I told her.

She handed the phone to me. "Call," she said. "You want to."

Soon as she said it, I knew she was right. And it gave me a strange feeling to think she knew what was in my head. Not that I would admit it. "What if I don't call?" I said.

"They'll come looking for you."

"They'll never find me," I said.

"You told your father my name. You mustn't be found here."

"Why not?"

"Call," she said.

I dialed. The phone rang just once.

"Hello!" It was Aunt Lu.

"Aunt Lu—" I began.

"Conrad!" she shouted instantly. "Where are you? I've been *desperate* with worry. Did you miss your plane? Did the stewardess lose you? Were you sick? I have to know, honey. Where are you now?"

"I'm in New York City. Staying with a friend."

"Aren't you calling from your mother's?"

89

"I don't know where she is."

"Haven't you spoken to her at all?"

"I tried, Aunt Lu. She wasn't home."

"Well, where are you now, honey? With what friend is that?"

"Just a friend."

"Give me his phone number so I can know where you are."

I didn't know what to say.

"Conrad," she said carefully, "listen to me. I must speak to his parents. I *must* thank them for all the help they've been giving you, what with your missing your plane like that. Put them on, honey, but make sure you come back and talk to me."

I lowered the receiver from my ear and covered the speaking part. "She wants to speak to your parents," I said to Nancy.

Nancy shook her head quickly.

"Aunt Lu," I said. "They aren't here."

"Conrad," she said, and I could hear the strain in her voice, "I want you to give me the number you are calling from. You hear? *Give it to me right this second!*"

"I'm all right, Aunt Lu, really I am."

"Conrad, I am trying to keep my self-control. I don't want to say things I'll be sorry for. Now you *must* give me your number. Do you hear me, you must—"

I hung up.

"Call your mother," Nancy said right away.

"Tomorrow," I said.

Pulling the phone toward her, Nancy dialed. She didn't even have to look at my paper. From the way she listened I could tell she was only getting the recording.

"Wouldn't it be weird," I said, "if she really was in Hollywood."

We sat there in the kitchen, neither of us saying anything, just sitting. My mind was replaying what I had heard my Aunt Lu saying on my mother's phone. Nothing was the way it was supposed to be. Everyone was different than I had thought.

I turned to Nancy. She was looking at me, her hands folded together on the table. I wasn't too sure I wanted to know what was going on in her head right then. So, I got up and drifted into the living room. Pat and her friend were still playing cards.

Pat was all dressed up, wearing a red silky shirt and matching pants, and shiny red sandals with high heels. She had lots of bracelets on her arms, and lipstick as red as her clothes. That, her short blonde hair, the red nail polish on her fingers and toes, all made her look strange. I think she must have done something to her face, too, like powdering it, because it looked very white, almost chalky. She reminded me of something out of a horror show.

The guy was very different. He was wearing a neat, ordinary suit, vest, and tie. His shoes were polished. I liked his mustache, which was long, curved, carefully trimmed. He looked like he knew exactly what he was doing.

I sat on the floor and watched them play. They were both very serious, hardly looking at each other, just at their cards, as if the game was the most important thing in the world. But then suddenly Pat threw her cards down in a heap. "I'm *bored*," she announced.

The guy looked up, startled. "Hey," he said. "I had you beat."

"Maybe," she said. She got up and walked into her room, shutting the door behind her. The guy looked over his cards, then at hers, then shuffled them all together with his big hands. After a few moments of waiting he went and knocked on Pat's door. When she didn't answer, he tried the doorknob. She must have locked the door; he couldn't get it open. So he stood there, embarrassed, even more so when he turned and saw that I was watching him.

"Crazy," he said to me. "Very, very crazy. She had better cards than I did."

I didn't say anything. Nancy came into the room and sat at the table.

"You her brother?" the guy said to me.

I shook my head.

"What are you doing here, then?"

"I'm Nancy's husband," I said, pointing at her.

He looked at Nancy, then at me. "Right," he said. "And I'm Mr. Spock." He held out his hand, Vulcan style. "Tell her I've left, will you?" he said, nodding toward Pat's door. Then he walked out of the room and we heard the front door shut.

Pat came out of her room.

"He left," I told her.

She sat down, stretching her legs out in front of her, wiggling her toes. "You staying here again?" she asked me.

"I guess."

"Find your folks?"

"Just my father."

"Like it here better?"

I didn't answer.

"How many movies today, Nancy?" she asked.

"I was with Conrad."

"Who cleaned up this place?" she asked. "Was that you, Conrad?"

"Yeah."

"You're hired," she said, closing her eyes. "What did you mean by telling that guy you were Nancy's husband?"

"Just a joke," I said.

"I've heard worse," said Pat. "Just don't tell your in-laws upstairs. They won't laugh. Hey," she said, sitting up straight. "I forgot to ask that guy his name."

"Mr. Spock," I said.

"Figures," she said. After a while she got up and, without saying anything, went into her room and closed the door behind her. This time I could hear the lock turn.

Exhausted, I leaned back against the couch.

What I wanted to do most of all was sleep.

"Conrad," I heard Nancy say, "I think you should go back to St. Louis. Tomorrow."

I tried not to listen. I was sick of her telling me what to do, of everybody telling me what to do.

"Your mother might be gone for a while, and you aren't going to go see your father on Monday, are you?"

I didn't answer, annoyed that she knew what was in my head.

"Then you might as well go home."

"My ticket isn't till next weekend," I told her.

"You can change it."

"I want to see my mother first."

"What if she doesn't come back?"

I ignored the question.

"Well, what if she doesn't?"

"She has to come back sometime," I said.

"You should have told her you were coming. Your father, too."

"I couldn't."

"What would she have said if you had told her?"

"I don't know."

"Are you glad you came?"

"I don't know."

"Why do you keep saying that?"

"Because I *don't* know anything anymore! Besides," I said, "why should you care? You never say anything. You don't tell me what's on *your* mind." I sat up. "Yeah," I demanded, "what's in *your* head?"

She sat there staring at me, that frightened look on her face. Then she covered her face with her hands. That butterfly—it scared me.

Sunday Morning

When I woke the next morning my first thought was for my St. Louis home. I missed it. It was all so regular there. I could count on things. I knew what to do, what not to do, how my aunt and uncle would react. Since I had come to New York, nothing had worked that way at all. I was beginning to think Nancy was right—I should go back.

I got up, checked the time, saw that it was seven-thirty. Feeling grubby—I hadn't taken my clothes off since I'd left St. Louis—I decided to take a shower. Getting cleaned up made me feel better. Then, in the kitchen, I found a soft apple. Usually I hate them soft, but I ate it anyway.

I made myself sit down and try to think through what had happened. I couldn't. The only thing I knew was that I felt too cooped up. I decided to go out and take a walk.

When I left I jimmied the door lock with a folded piece of paper so the door couldn't shut completely. I even told the doorman I'd be back. I wasn't certain I was coming back—but I wanted to be sure I could get in if I did.

Outside the sky was clear, but pale. There was even a faint moon in the sky, a morning memory of itself. It reminded me of Sister Mary's face at Nancy's school—Sister Mary looking at me, wondering what I knew. Well, if she had asked me right then, I would have told her, "Nothing."

Across the way, where Central Park was, it was just green. Looking at the park, I remembered the couple I'd seen that first night—how long ago that seemed—the lady with the light green blouse and the pretty eyes. I wished I could see her again. She had looked so happy.

The streets were empty. Only a few cars were out. When I stood on the corner looking down Fifth Avenue I saw no one.

I wandered along, just thinking, thinking hard, because I knew I was scared. It wasn't a being-scared-of-the-dark kind of thing. Just the opposite. It was seeing everything clearly and not liking it.

Once Uncle Carl gave me a little calculator. You could add, subtract, do long division on it. It seemed simple. Then I dropped it, and all the insides spilled out. So many parts! When he got me a new one, even when I added two plus two I kept thinking of those insides. Two plus two wasn't simple anymore. That's the way I was feeling, that's the way I was scared—scared that nothing would ever be simple again.

I stopped. What I wanted to do was get back to the apartment—to Nancy.

Then I realized I was lost. Worse, nobody was there to ask for directions.

I made myself stand absolutely still, trying to go over in my mind which way I'd come. I even closed my eyes, but then opened them fast when I heard a scraping, scratching sound. I looked around, but couldn't tell where or what it was.

Then I saw. Across the street. The man I'd seen that first night, the blind man, the man with no legs sitting on a little cart with roller-skate wheels. He was pushing himself with his long, powerful arms and the wooden hammers. He went slowly, his head thrown back, his empty eyes looking for something. I wondered what he was seeing in his head. Then I remembered that I had promised myself that if I ever saw him again I would give him some money.

Still, I didn't move, I just watched as he pushed himself slowly, his body swaying, the little sign around his neck: I AM BLIND. GOD BLESS YOU!!! The American flag.

And I told myself again that I had promised to give him something, that I had to do it.

I ran across the street and up behind him. Hearing me, knowing I was there, he stopped and spun about. Petrified, I froze.

I was very frightened, suddenly feeling that he wasn't really blind, that he was looking at me, into me, that he might be able to hurt me. *But I had promised to give him something.* I couldn't move.

"Who's there?" he shouted in the empty street. His voice was high, not low the way I had thought it would be.

"Who's there?" he cried again. His face was dirty, he needed a shave. His clothes were soiled.

Even if I had known what to say, I don't think I could have spoken.

"Who's that? Who's that?" he said. Lifting an arm, he held one of the wooden hammers like a weapon.

I saw then that he was scared of me, even as I was of him. I had to do something to make him less frightened. It would help me, too.

"I want to give you something," I said.

"What?" he demanded.

"Money."

He didn't move the arm with the hammer, but with his other hand he took up his cup and held it out, rattling the coins inside. He tried to smile; his body danced. It was so ugly. I had to force myself not to back away.

Slowly, I walked toward him. When I got up close I could smell him. He stank. I got out the rest of my money, all of it, more than twenty dollars in bills, and stuffed it into his cup.

Puzzlement came over his face. He dropped

the hammer to the ground and his hand went to the bills, plucking them out of the cup. He rubbed them between his fingers, then against his rough cheek.

"God bless you!" he suddenly shouted, as if I were a mile away, not just two feet. When I didn't answer, he shouted it again, screaming, "*God bless you!*"

I turned and ran, ran as fast as I could. At the corner I caught a glimpse of green. It was the park. I fled back to the apartment.

I made myself some breakfast. But after that I could only wait around, because Nancy was still asleep. I lay on the couch, thinking about nothing in particular—about New York City, the St. Louis Cardinals, places where my mother might be, my father, who he was going out with, St. Louis again, the Gateway Arch that I had flown over. I felt I really wanted to see it again— to get home, where things were all under control.

Even as I had that thought, a new idea got into my head: maybe St. Louis wasn't so simple either.

It was too much to think about. I shut my eyes on that one.

I must have fallen asleep, because the next thing I knew Nancy was up, walking around. She didn't pay any attention to me. I watched her, thinking how strange it was that she, someone I had met by accident, was so important to me, that I was in her house and glad to be there. Then she turned and saw me looking at her.

"I still have the copy of *True Romances*," I said. "What do you want me to do with it?"

"Nothing."

"You never finished reading it."

"It's stupid."

"Then why were you reading it?"

She shrugged. "The same reason I watch movies."

"What would have happened if your school had found you reading it?"

"Nothing. A talking-to."

"Then why didn't you want it there?"

"I didn't want them to know I read stuff like that."

"There are a lot of things you don't want people to know, aren't there?" I said.

"Maybe."

"It's under my mattress in St. Louis," I told her.

"When I get back," she said, "we can meet there and I'll read it."

It was the first time I had heard her say something that was supposed to be funny. I smiled.

"Do they let visitors come to your school?" I asked.

"Only family and friends."

"Does that include husbands?"

"Are you going to call your mother?"

"I guess."

She started to go for her phone, but stopped. She had made up her mind about something, I could see that. She said, "Pat and I are supposed to have dinner upstairs with my mother and father tonight."

"That's all right."

"I want you to come."

"Why?" I asked.

Instead of answering, she brought out her phone and placed it on the floor next to me. By that time I knew my mom's phone number by heart, so I just dialed, Nancy watching all the time.

The phone rang twice. "Hello?" said a sleepy voice. It was my mother, for real. I knew it right off.

"Mom?" I said.

"Conrad?" Her voice was completely awake. "Is that you, Conrad?"

"Hi," I said.

"Where are you?" she said.

"With a friend."

"Conrad, people are absolutely frantic about you. Your Aunt Lu is threatening to come here if she doesn't hear from you again. She's saying all these terrible things. And your father . . . Are you close by? You've done a terrible thing, Conrad. You can't just decide to come like this. Conrad, are you listening to me?"

I was trying not to, but I said, "Yes."

"Where are you now?" she asked.

"I told you, with a friend."

"I'll come and get you."

"I'll come there," I said, and I hung up quickly.

"Where was she?" asked Nancy.

"I didn't ask."

"Are you going to see her?"

"I guess."

"Is she angry?"

"Yes."

"You should go anyway."

"You going to come with me?"

She didn't answer right away. Then: "Do you want me to?"

"Yeah."

"Why?"

"I'm afraid to go alone," I admitted. "Please?"

For a long time she sat there saying nothing. Once, twice I thought she was going to say something. But in the end all she did say was "Okay," as if it had taken her that long to get the message from wherever she got messages from.

. . .

Sunday Afternoon

The taxi went through the city fast, too fast. I sat slumped in one corner, Nancy in the other. From time to time she looked at me.

"I don't have any money," I said.

"That's all right," she said, putting out her hand, her butterfly hand, to touch mine.

The street where my mother lived looked just the same as it had before—narrow, with the small, thin-bark trees with their new, half-dead leaves. As far as I was concerned I could have stayed in the taxi and gone back.

However, Nancy paid the driver and he went off.

I stood there, my heart beating too fast, not wanting anything to go wrong, trying to get up the nerve to move. Nancy waited patiently. Then I saw that she was just as scared as I was; that actually made me feel better. I was able to make myself go into the house and push the button under my mother's mailbox. Almost instantly there was an answering buzz. Up we went, Nancy making sure I led the way.

When I reached the second floor I looked up the stairs, half expecting to see my mother waiting. When she wasn't, I felt disappointed. We kept on going until we reached her door, and I knocked.

"Come in!"

I opened the door—and could not believe what I saw. It was my mother, all dressed up in a costume, an Uncle Sam costume, with red-and-white striped pants, a string tie, and a high hat studded with stars. Hanging from her chin was this phony-looking, scraggly goat beard.

She was sitting beside, or behind, or in this thing: a bass drum with bells hanging on it, as well as balloons of all colors, and three squeeze horns, too. In one hand she held a big drumstick that was streaming with ribbons. In the other hand she had a silver trumpet. On her arms were jingle bells.

The moment we walked in she called out, "Welcome, Conrad!" And she began to play, began to play everything at once. The drum began to beat, the bells to jangle, the horns to bleat, the trumpet to sound. It was like an explosion. And it seemed as if she was dancing, too, because she had to jump up and down and wave her hands as she beat the drum, blew the horn, and did all the rest.

The noise got louder and louder. I felt stunned. I turned to look at Nancy. Her eyes were open very wide.

"Welcome, Conrad!" my mother called again. "And now for our second number. 'When Conrad Comes Marching Home Again!' " And while we stood there she started a whole new song.

It went on and on until we heard a voice bellowing from somewhere in the house: "Shut up, for Christ's sake! It's Sunday!"

My mother stopped and looked at me with a big smile. She wasn't a very big woman; her arms and hands were slim, her eyes bright, laughing. Her blonde, curly hair seemed pretty to me, as always, and her quick movements were full of excitement. "What do you think?" she said.

"About what?" I somehow got out.

"The getup."

"I don't know."

"It's for Culver cigarettes. New product. Conrad, your mother is the one and only Culver Cigarette One-Person Band!" She held out her arms. "Going to give the Culver Cigarette One-Person Band a hug and a kiss?"

I hung back.

"What's the matter?" she teased. "Don't you kiss ladies with beards?" She looked toward Nancy. "Shut the door, honey, will you?"

Nancy did.

"You going to introduce me to your girl friend, Conrad?"

"I tried to call, but you weren't here," I said, ignoring her question.

"I know. Bob told me you even came over here. But I've been working all the time, honey. Here. There. Everywhere. Yesterday I was at a new shopping mall in Worcester. That's in Massachusetts. Dreadful place! Honey, you weren't worried about me, were you?" She put down her things, and, taking off her beard, came out from behind the band stuff, reached for me, and gave me a big hug and a kiss on the head.

"Sooooo good to see you!" she said, taking my hand and drawing me over to a chair. She sat, making me stand in front of her.

"Conrad, honey," she said softly, "what in God's good name are you doing here?" Her eyes were no longer laughing.

"I came to see you," I said.

"I guess you have," she said. Then she snatched up a cigarette, lit it, threw herself back in the chair. "You're as crazy as your mom, did you know that?" She reached forward and mussed my hair. "You weren't supposed to be here, that's for sure. When Lu told me you were going to England I was so *happy* for you. I mean, I was so afraid you'd want to come here and I'd have to say no. But she told me you wanted to go there.

"Now let me tell you something," my mother said. "Aunt Lu is about to kill us both. When she gets on the warpath . . . Let me look at you!" She pushed me to arm's length and studied me.

"Handsomer. Bigger. You're looking sooooo good, Conrad!

"Now, you don't have to say a thing," she went on. "Sister Lu, in fifteen messages, costing I hate to think how much, told me exactly what happened: how you missed your plane because of some stupid, ignorant stewardess. How you got scared. How you tried to reach her, and me, and your father, and the Lord knows who else. . . . How is your father?"

"Okay."

"I'm glad you saw him. Poor man. He still calls me. But then, everybody calls me except casting directors. *I* have to call *them*. Always."

She brushed some hair off my forehead. "It takes my boy to miss an airplane to England. I never did like to fly. Makes me sooooo nervous. I have to steer those planes myself, up *and* down. And the little bitty planes I fly! Still, it works better than a diet. I don't *dare* eat. First thing I do when I get on a plane is tie on the seat belt with a square knot, then check out the barf bag." She laughed, scrunching up her face.

"Are you acting?" I asked.

" 'Are you acting?' he asks. Honey, I'm *not* exactly your dyed-in-the-wool true-blue Uncle Sam. It's exposure, though. What I'm hoping is that it will lead to a TV commercial. I did a test for one and they actually tried it out. Lots of money in that kind of thing, *real* money. That's what they tell me, anyway. I never see the stuff."

"Why didn't you want me to come here?" I asked.

She looked at me. "Conrad," she said, "you *wanted* to go to England."

"Did *you* want me to go there?" I asked.

"What do you mean, honey?"

"I wanted to come here."

She looked at me very hard, then put her hands on either side of my face. "I know," she said at last, her voice very low.

"I could have helped with the band," I said.

She said, "Then it wouldn't have been a one-person band, would it?"

Suddenly, she became very busy. "As soon as I heard you were here," she said, "I flew out to get stuff for brunch—orange juice, English muffins, jam, cornflakes. . . . Whatever you see, you can have. Hungry?" All the while she was talking she was setting up a little table and putting things on it.

"Aren't you even going to tell me her name?" she asked, nodding toward Nancy.

"I'm sorry," I said, having completely forgotten. "This is Nancy."

"Hello, Nancy. You sit, too."

But there were only two chairs. My mother had to pick up the table and move it toward the couch so a third person could sit there. I started to help, only she wanted to do it by herself. But when she moved the table, the bottle of juice slid off and smashed on the floor.

"Oh my God!" my mother screamed. She

rushed into the bathroom and came back with a big bath towel. Then she sat on the floor, trying to soak up the mess. The next moment she stopped. There was an awful silence.

She had her back to me, but I could see that she was shaking. Then I realized she was crying. I didn't know what to do.

"Conrad?" Her back was still to me.

"What?"

"It's such a mess, isn't it?"

"It's okay," I said. "We don't need the juice."

She shook her head very hard. "Not that. I knew you wanted to come here, but this crazy thing . . . There's no time, no place, no . . . But you love me anyway, don't you? In spite of all this craziness, you do love me. I know you do. Say you love me. Please, I need to know that."

"Sure," I got out.

She turned around, reached out, and hugged me, hugged me so hard it hurt. For a long time we just stayed that way. Then she let me go, shook her head, and laughed. "Hell of a way to eat breakfast, isn't it?" she said, getting up.

We sat at the table. My mother insisted on taking the couch, which was so low it made her look like a midget. She just laughed, smoked, and talked.

She told us all about her travels for the cigarette people, what happened, who she met, how once she had been interviewed for a TV news story in Wheeling, West Virginia. How her theater agent thought she would be getting a real break soon. On and on she went, hardly stopping, smoking a lot, laughing even more, with the kind of laugh that makes you laugh, too—you can't help it. We ate some, but mostly we listened.

Then she said, "Aunt Lu will come, Conrad. You have to tell me where you're staying so she can get in touch with you."

I stole a look at Nancy. "Is she really coming?" I wanted to know.

"She said so. And she is sooooo angry, Conrad. I can't take her when she's angry, going on about what she does for me, how she isn't appreciated. . . . What are we going to do?"

"Tell her she doesn't have to come."

"What do you mean?" said my mother, alarmed. "Conrad, I have to fly to Albany. Soon. I have to."

"I'll go back," I said. "I can do it myself."

"Could you?" said my mother, relieved. "Is that what you want to do? For sure?"

I nodded.

"Conrad," she said, "the *last* thing I need in my life right now is big sister Lu handing me a list of my faults. 'Now, honey,' " she said, imitating Aunt Lu, " 'you're a *lovely* girl, but your head is just *full* of cotton candy. . . . ' I can't take it, Conrad, not now. Anyway, this trip I'm supposed to take, that I'm going to take—it could be very important. I—"

"Tell her I'm coming," I said.

"Conrad, *you* tell her. You'd do it much better

than me. And it'll make her feel good."

"Okay," I said.

"And it's all right for you to stay with Nancy and her parents?"

"Nancy doesn't live with her parents."

"Oh?"

"With her sister."

"Thank *heaven* for sisters! Nancy, please *do* tell your sister how *much* I appreciate it. How did you two meet?"

"In St. Louis," I said.

"Don't tell me," my mother cried. "By the great arch. I've heard of it. How romantic!"

We talked some more, but it was just talk. We weren't listening to each other, and anyway, my mother kept looking at the clock. Finally, I told her we had to go. She gave me some more hugs.

"Tell me when you're coming next time, honey, and I'll try, try, *try*—Girl Scout's honor—to be here. I really promise I'll try."

"That's okay," I told her.

"Want to hear some music as you go? 'Hail to the Chief'? They do it for all the Presidents."

"It'll bother your neighbors," I reminded her.

Sunday Evening

When we got outside I realized I felt lousy. My head hurt. My insides were tangled. "I guess I shouldn't have come," I said. "I mean, Aunt Lu and Uncle Carl were probably right not to want me to. I guess they were protecting me. . . . Maybe I should get my ticket changed and go. When do you get back to St. Louis?"

"In another week. Next Sunday."

"That's a lot of movies," I said.

We were lucky and found a taxi quick. Halfway back to the apartment Nancy took my hand and held it with both of hers. It made me feel better.

When we got there Pat was watching a tennis match on TV. I waited in the kitchen for Nancy to bring her phone. I dialed St. Louis, and Uncle Carl answered.

"Uncle Carl, this is Conrad."

"Conrad! Good grief, boy, you've put us through all the hoops and that's no mistake. What's come over you? Where the hell are you?"

"New York."

"Your mother's?"

"Uncle Carl, I wanted to tell you I'm coming back."

"Your Aunt Lu will be glad to hear that. She's sleeping now—she hasn't slept the last two nights. Conrad, let me tell you, that woman has been hurt by all this, deeply hurt. But bless her, she's a forgiving soul. I know, believe me. She'll forgive you, too. You can count on it. When do you get back, boy?"

"I'm not sure. I have to change the ticket. I'll let you know. Tell her I'll make it as soon as possible. She shouldn't come here. I'll get back on my own."

"Do that and everything will be fine, Conrad. I know you can do it. Call us as soon as you know your arrival time. Your Aunt Lu will be sitting right by the phone. And, Conrad, say hello to your mother!"

I thought he would talk some more, but instead, he hung up. Still, short as the conversation had been, it had taken the rest of my energy. I felt so tired, so awful—worse and worse every minute. For a while all I could do was rest my head on my arms.

When I looked up, Pat was leaning against the kitchen doorway. She looked different, not

114

nearly so crazy as before. In fact, she looked almost normal.

"We're supposed to go upstairs," she said to Nancy. "Din-din."

"I asked Conrad to come," said Nancy.

"Are you serious?" Pat asked, surprised.

"Yes."

Pat looked at me. "He doesn't look so great," she said, sounding worried.

"I don't think I should go," I said quickly. "I don't feel like eating anyway."

"I want you to see them," said Nancy.

"Why?" I asked, trying to read her thoughts.

As usual, she wouldn't let me. All she said was, "It's important to me."

I didn't know what she meant, but I couldn't refuse, not after what I had been asking her to do for me. So I went into the bathroom, washed my face, combed my hair, fixed my tie. I didn't think I looked very decent—I was still feeling crummy—but Nancy said I looked okay.

She had gotten dressed in her school uniform, and looked exactly the same as when I'd first seen her, right to the dumb teddy bear pin on her collar. It was like a disguise.

While we waited for the elevator, Pat suddenly said, "Conrad, I don't know what kind of parents you have, but ours . . . well, they have their own rules. If you talk, be careful. They don't have to know everything."

"I don't want to say anything," I told her, and I meant it.

115

We went up a good number of floors—to the top. Then we got out into this little hall. On Nancy's floor, when you got out of the elevator, you saw doors to lots of different apartments. On that floor there was only one door.

Pat, acting nervous, knocked. A woman in a white uniform opened the door. The girls went in, and I followed.

We passed by a couple of rooms. Right off I could see how rich Nancy's parents were. It didn't feel like an apartment at all. It wasn't only that everything seemed very expensive—rugs, paintings on the wall, stuff like that—it was that the place seemed too perfect, with no feeling that anybody actually lived there. It felt like one of those model rooms in a department store.

And all of a sudden I was scared.

We went into a large room, the fanciest of all. The Sperlings were waiting for us, perfectly posed. I don't think they moved a hair when we came in.

Mrs. Sperling, sitting in a big chair, was dressed as if she was going out to a fancy place, not staying home for dinner. Everything about her was supersmooth—her hair, her skin, even the clothes she wore. Nothing was out of place. She probably thought "wrinkle" was a dirty word. Her hands were as still as pieces of white stone. Even her smile showed perfect teeth. She looked like an advertisement, except I didn't know what she was selling.

Sitting behind her at a table was Mr. Sperling, Nancy's father, wearing a dark suit with a vest. He looked big, not so much strong as thick, with a perfectly smooth, round, bright pink face, hair carefully combed. He just looked forward, neither smiling nor frowning, the tips of his fingers tapping on the tabletop like a slow clock.

We stood at the door.

"Good evening, dears," said Mrs. Sperling, not moving, only tilting her head up. Pat, then Nancy, went up and kissed her on the cheek, as if it was some kind of ceremony. Mrs. Sperling kissed the air. After going to Mr. Sperling for the same business, the girls sat down and waited.

After a moment Mrs. Sperling said, "Are you going to tell me your friend's name?"

"Conrad," said Pat.

"Conrad who?"

"Buckingham," Pat said.

Mrs. Sperling still hadn't actually looked at me. "Were you intending to invite Conrad for dinner?" she asked.

"I insisted." Pat answered again, as if by keeping Nancy and me from talking she was protecting us.

"I think we can manage," said Mrs. Sperling.

And then—we just waited, I didn't know for what, or whom. I mean, I kept thinking that someone was about to speak, had to, but it didn't happen. The four of them just sat there, not moving, silent. And it wasn't a regular silence. It was alive, crawling over everything, squeezing the air out of the room, pushing itself into every corner, into mouths, ears, making the smallest sounds seem loud.

Mr. Sperling, slowly tapping his fingers.

Pat, sitting straight, showing nothing of her thoughts, just the small part of a smile.

Mrs. Sperling, not a muscle moving, not a hair moving.

Nancy, staring in front of her, the zombie look.

And always the silence, so heavy and thick, and the waiting, the constant waiting for something to happen.

Then, out of nowhere, Mrs. Sperling was talking to me. "Conrad," she said, "tell us about yourself. Where is your home?"

It caught me completely by surprise. By then I wasn't expecting her to say anything, certainly not to talk to me, not to ask that. I didn't know how to answer, couldn't begin to speak.

I turned to Nancy. She wouldn't even look at me. I glanced at Pat. She shook her head, just enough to remind me of what she had said at the elevator, that I had to be careful. I felt panicky, trapped, didn't know what to do.

Turning back to Mrs. Sperling, I tried desperately to find an answer, some clue to what I should say.

"Conrad, where is your home?" repeated Mrs. Sperling.

I felt I had no choice. I did what I had always

done—I lied. "I live in New York," I began slowly, trying to find my way. "But I go to school in St. Louis. The best boys' one. I met Nancy at a dance at St. Agnes. My parents are pretty important people. My father works for the mayor. My mother raises lots of money for hospitals."

I said it without once daring to look at Mrs. Sperling, ashamed of saying it, feeling dirty with the lying, the faking, certain she had to know that none of it was true.

But all she said was, "I see."

I looked to Pat. She nodded. To Nancy. Nothing.

"Have you had a pleasant vacation?" asked Mrs. Sperling.

"Yes, ma'am," I managed to get out.

"You've had good weather," she said.

"Yes, ma'am," I said again.

Then the silence came back, that awful silence that seemed to just take over.

In that silence I kept hearing what I had said—heard it repeating itself over and over again like a stuck record. I wanted it to stop. I didn't want to say things like that anymore. I was sick of that kind of lying. I wished I could say something real.

But the silence was too big.

Mr. Sperling broke into it by saying, "What have you been doing, Nancy?"

Nancy answered so softly I almost couldn't hear her. "Reading," she whispered. "And going to museums, and doing my schoolwork."

"Nancy is a very hardworking student," Mrs. Sperling said to me. "At the top of her class. Isn't that so, Nancy?"

Nancy didn't answer.

"Nancy?" her mother prompted, a little edge to her voice.

"Yes," Nancy agreed. "That's true."

I had been feeling bad before, but by now I was beginning to feel crazy, too. I mean, the silence was bad enough, but when we spoke nobody said anything that was real—not them, not me, no one.

"It's nice to have the girls here," Mrs. Sperling continued.

Then, again, silence, silence until Mrs. Sperling said, "Nancy, please tell Alice to set another place at the table. We should go in to dinner soon."

Nancy, zombie expression in place, left the room. The moment she was gone, Mrs. Sperling turned to me. "We're very fond of our Nancy."

"Yes," said Mr. Sperling. "We're very lucky in both our daughters."

Mrs. Sperling stood then, and smoothed her already smooth skirt. It was she who led the way to the dining room. Mr. Sperling and Pat followed.

I stayed where I was, trying to find an excuse not to go, not wanting to be there or hear any more, not the words, not the silence.

But, hearing something, I looked up. Nancy had come back. She was standing there, waiting for me, looking so careful in her uniform, her eyeglass frames pink in the light, the teddy bear pin sitting on her collar. Looking at her, I thought for a moment that they really did know who she was, that it was me who didn't know her. But as she stood there I saw that she was rubbing her hand, the butterfly.

I knew then that there was more, and that I had to go through with it.

On the table were a tablecloth and places laid out with all kinds of plates, silver, fancy glass, big cloth napkins. I had never seen anything like it before—not in a house, anyway.

Mrs. Sperling took a chair at one end of the table and Mr. Sperling sat at the other. "Conrad," she said, indicating a chair next to her. I sat down, across from Nancy.

"Thomas," Mrs. Sperling said to Mr. Sperling, "will you say grace?"

When they put their hands in their laps and bowed their heads I did the same. Mr. Sperling said a prayer. It was all about thanking the Lord that they were still together as a loving family, that the love they had for each other was as much as they had for God. Something like that.

He had hardly hit the "Amen" button when the maid came in and placed a cup of fruit in front of each of us. But no one did or said anything, not until Mrs. Sperling picked up her spoon, the signal that we could begin.

I had to make myself eat. It wasn't just my

insides, either. My hand was shaking. What I really wanted to do was get out of there, lie down, get rid of the pain that was building in my head. I still hadn't stopped hearing what I had said about myself—all those stupid lies. And I kept asking myself why I had told them, why I couldn't have told the truth for once. In the midst of all that I heard the careful clicking of spoons against dishes, against perfect teeth, the sound of sucking lips.

Nobody said a word. They just went on, like each one was in a separate box, until I couldn't take it anymore. Until, in that silence, I heard a voice—it was my voice—and my voice was saying, "I don't live with my parents."

For a moment no one said anything. Then Mrs. Sperling said, "I beg your pardon?"

"I don't live with my parents," I repeated, louder.

"I see," said Mrs. Sperling, and she resumed eating.

"*I don't live with my parents!*" I said a third time, almost shouting.

Mrs. Sperling took a quick look at her husband, then said, "Whom do you live with, then?"

"My aunt and uncle."

She considered that. "That's interesting," she said, and took another spoonful of fruit.

"My parents live in New York," I went on. "But they're divorced."

"Conrad," said Mr. Sperling, "it's not necessary for you to go into the details—"

"It *is* necessary," I said, looking across at Nancy, who was staring straight down at her plate.

"Oh?" said Mrs. Sperling.

"Because it's true," I said. "My parents live in New York. I live in St. Louis. I go to a regular school."

"I see," said Mrs. Sperling. She put down her spoon, started to say something else, stopped, picked up her spoon again.

"My father doesn't work for the mayor," I went on. "My mother doesn't raise money for hospitals."

Mrs. Sperling turned from me to Pat, then back to me again. "I am confused," she said, trying to make a joke of it. "Am I to believe what you are saying now, or what you said before?"

"My father sells furniture at Macy's," I continued.

"Interesting," said Mr. Sperling flatly, as he wiped his hands with his napkin.

"What subjects have you been studying most of all?" Mrs. Sperling said to Nancy.

"It *isn't* interesting," I cut in "It's *stupid.* And my father knows it's stupid. He hates it. He wants to be an actor. But he can't. He doesn't know what to do."

Mr. Sperling flexed his hands into fists. "Look here, Conrad, you're right. We're *not* interested in these personal things about you. After all—"

"*But it's true!*" I shouted, and it was like an alarm going off in my head. For, building inside

123

of me, from no place I had ever been before, no place I had ever looked before, was an explosion. The only thing I could feel was how angry I was—at my aunt, my uncle, my mother, my father, at everyone I had ever lied to, at everyone who had let me lie. I was angry at myself, too, because I had let myself lie, had told myself lies. I never told the truth—not about what I saw, thought, or felt. I was so afraid of the truth, afraid of what it would do to me, that I felt I had to lie. But things had gotten so bad that lying wouldn't help. I was going to tell the truth now, no matter what.

"My father's no good at anything," I said. "No good at all."

"Well, really . . ." said Mrs. Sperling. She seemed to move a little farther away from me.

I turned to her. "Do you know what my mother does?" I demanded.

Mrs. Sperling, staring at me, only shook her head.

"She's a one-person band for a cigarette," I said.

"For a cigarette?" she repeated.

"She's good at it. The best in the world. The only one in the world. She's so good at it that she doesn't have time to see me."

"Forgive me," said Mrs. Sperling. "I really don't care for this. Patricia," she said, "is this boy one of your bad jokes?"

Mr. Sperling flipped his napkin onto the table. "Mr. Buckingham," he said, "this really is quite enough. We don't wish to hear any more. Do I make myself clear? No more!"

"I'm talking!" I shouted, freezing them in their places. "And my name's not Buckingham. It's Murray. And do you know why I live with my aunt and uncle instead of with my parents?" I said. Now I was crying, unable to stop.

"Because my parents can't have me with them. Because they don't know how. Because there's no room for me. Because I'd be in the way. Because they don't need me. Because I'd only make life harder for them. Because they don't want me to see how much they don't like themselves. Because they don't have the time to love me and they can't stand the way it makes them feel!"

Mrs. Sperling turned to Nancy. "Do you understand what this is all about?"

Nancy, refusing to look at me, only shook her head violently, saying no.

"I didn't think so," said Mrs. Sperling. "I find this very unappetizing."

"She *does* understand!" I said. "She knows it's true!"

"I don't care *what* it is," said Mrs. Sperling. "I would think you could find some measure of self-control in a place where you have been made to feel welcome. That's common politeness. But perhaps it's fortunate you are here, among a family that live normal lives. Our family is together. We care for one another."

And I said, "No you don't! How could you?

You don't even live together. You don't know anything about Nancy."

Mrs. Sperling pushed out her chair and stood up. "I am sorry. I do not wish to hear any more!"

"Why? Because I know her? Because I care about her?" I said, looking straight at Nancy.

"This is quite enough," said Mrs. Sperling.

"*Listen to me!*" I cried.

Mr. Sperling, very red in the face, leaned forward toward me. "Damn it, boy, you are an invited guest in this house. If you can't control yourself—"

"Nancy and I don't lie to each other," I said.

"Leave this house!" said Mr. Sperling.

"We like each other," I said. "We help each other. We love each other."

"Get out!" said Mr. Sperling. "Get out before I throw you out!"

But I was watching Nancy. She was sitting absolutely rigid, staring, not at me, but at the plate in front of her, with that dead, dead look of hers, refusing to hear me.

I began to shout at her. "Look at me!" I yelled. "You know what I'm saying is true. You know it is! You know it as much as me! Why won't you say what you feel? Look at me!" I screamed. "*Say what you feel!*" And, leaning forward, I swept away everything from in front of her, so that all the dishes, glasses, the little cups of fruit, everything, went flying off in all directions.

Mr. Sperling leaped to his feet, sending his chair crashing backward. Brushing himself off

126

frantically, swearing, he stormed out of the room.

"Young man," said Mrs. Sperling, her face livid, "you are not wanted here. And you are to have nothing to do with Nancy. Do you understand me? *Nothing*. I insist upon that. Nancy, I forbid you to be with him!" Then she left the room, too.

I just sat there, shaking, crying, trying to hold on.

I had to get into the air. Pat got us outside. "Take a walk," she said. "Stay lost for a few hours."

When we got to the sidewalk it was already dark. "Can we go into the park?" I asked.

"Too dangerous at night," Nancy said.

We started to walk. I was so shocked by what I had done that I was trembling. I didn't know what was going to happen. And I didn't know what Nancy was feeling, either. That was what worried me most.

"I had to say those things," I managed to get out. "I had to."

Nancy, not saying anything, just stared straight ahead.

We kept walking. It was Sunday night, so Fifth Avenue was pretty deserted, except for some empty buses that went roaring by. Only a few office lights were on. In the store windows the dummies stood like frozen people. Way downtown we could see the Empire State Building, lights blazing like fire on a mountaintop.

Then all of a sudden I stopped and turned to Nancy. "Why did you want me to see them?" I said. "What was the point of it? I don't understand. It doesn't make any sense. Tell me what's going on. *Please*. I have to know!"

For a long time she looked at me, not saying anything, looking at me with those same eyes I had seen at her school in St. Louis, eyes showing nothing but pain. Then she lifted her hand, slowly, her right hand, and held it in front of her face. I saw it again, on the back of her hand: the tiny green butterfly tattoo.

"I don't understand," I said, bewildered. "I don't."

"It's me," she whispered in a voice that almost wasn't there. "Nothing else is."

"That doesn't make any sense," I said.

"Everything else is dead," she said.

"What do you mean?" I asked, horrified.

Still she stood there looking at me, the hand up, and I understood for the first time that it wasn't that she didn't want to tell me—she just couldn't.

"Try to tell me," I begged. "You have to. Please."

Then, slowly at first, she did begin to talk, trying to find words. Sometimes she looked at me, sometimes not. Her voice was loud one moment, so soft the next I almost couldn't hear her. All of it came as if she were running here, there, everywhere, instead of standing still, as she truly was. I don't even know how long it took her to say it all. But she said it. And I listened.

"My parents used to fight," she said. "Not with their hands. With words. And with silence. All the time. It took me a very long time, but then I found a way . . . to tell them . . . that they should go away, from each other. It made them angry when I said that. They couldn't, they said. Why not? I asked. Because of me, they said. Other parents went apart. Not them. They accepted their duty, their responsibility, their choice. People in their position had to set an example.

"Then I knew that it was my fault . . . that if I wasn't around, things would be better. I thought about it, thought all the time, trying to find some way, any way, of freeing them. I thought of running away. Of killing myself. But I was too frightened to do those things.

"One day I was walking in the park. A butterfly went by. I reached out, tried to catch it. It only darted away. I ran after it, but always it flew out of reach. And when I gave up at last, the butterfly flew away, free, impossible to catch. But it gave me my idea.

"I'd turn myself into a butterfly. I really wanted to. Not that I could, of course. But I wanted to. What I did was go to a place where they did tattoos. I asked the man to put a green butterfly on my hand.

"Then I said to myself, the butterfly is me. I kill the rest. I won't see, or feel, or say anything.

No one will be able to touch what is really me.

"I never told my parents that. I only said it didn't matter what they did, I'd do only what they wanted me to do.

"They got frightened. They didn't know what to do—keep me near them or get rid of me. Every time they saw me, they got all upset. First they tried the separate apartment. Even that was too close. That's when they sent me to St. Louis. Still, they want people to think they like me. That's why I come home. But, you see, not too close.

"I saw your parents. You think what you have is bad, and maybe it is. But being together isn't always right either. My parents don't like each other, or care about anything. It's all pretending. None of it is real.

"The main thing is, no one can touch or have the part of me that's alive—unless I want them to."

When Nancy was done talking, I didn't know what to say, wasn't even sure what to feel. We started walking again. I felt as if we were the only ones in the whole city, as if the people, all those millions and millions and millions of people, were afraid to come out—afraid of us.

"It seems pretty nice out where you are in St. Louis," I said at last.

"Mostly they let me alone," Nancy said.

"That's because you don't talk much. I do. I'd probably hate it."

"I don't think you talk too much. . . . And I like

130

what you say," she added, taking my hand and holding it tight.

"I'd like to go to the top of the Empire State Building," I announced.

We stood on the observation deck at the top of the Empire State Building, looking out over the city. Clouds were actually below us, swirling around as a thin whiteness, so sometimes we could see the city, sometimes not—it was like a dream that came and went. For a long time we just watched.

"This is like being on the top of that arch in St. Louis," Nancy said at last. "It makes you feel small. But if you stand at the bottom of the arch, it's different. The arch goes so high, like two hands reaching up, trying to touch. You want to reach up with it, and sometimes you can."

Then she held out her hand, and there was the green butterfly dancing through the night. I held my hand out next to hers, and our two hands were like the two wings of a butterfly—a new butterfly—flying free.

I had pushed aside how I was feeling, but by the time we got back to Nancy's apartment there was no way I could pretend I wasn't sick. Absolutely numb, all I could do was sit on the couch with my eyes closed, holding on.

"Should I call a doctor?" Nancy asked.

"No," I told her. "I just want to get back to St. Louis."

Pat came and looked at me. Then they went into the kitchen and talked in low voices. Pat asked me for my plane ticket and my list of phone numbers. I gave it to her and she made some phone calls. When she was done she came back and sat next to me.

"Conrad," she said, "you can fly out of here tomorrow morning. Same airline. Just hand in your old ticket and tell them your name. Kennedy Airport. Ten o'clock in the morning. It's all taken care of. I even got you a window seat. And I called your people in St. Louis. They'll be waiting for you."

I sat there, shivering, feeling colder and colder.

"Put him to bed," said Pat. "I'll sleep out here."

I'm not quite sure what happened next. They took me into a bedroom, pulled off my shoes and jacket, and put me into bed, put covers over me. Not even that made me warmer.

I kept having these bad feelings, kept hearing things, kept seeing things. The whole trip, everything that had happened, replayed in my mind again and again. I couldn't get rid of it.

"Nancy!" I called. She came quickly, sat down on the bed near me.

"It's all so bad," I said, "None of it goes away."

After a moment she lay down next to me, and hugged me. We lay that way in the dark, feeling so close, peaceful.

The bad feelings began to go. I fell asleep.

Monday

It was seven when I woke. I remembered right away that I was supposed to get to the airport and to the plane. Looking over, I saw that Nancy was right there, sleeping.

I looked at her face. It was so different—quiet, soft, pretty.

I started to wake her, but changed my mind. The truth was, I wasn't sure that if she got up I would go. And I knew that I had to go, myself, with no help from her. I had to.

So I let her sleep.

I found my jacket, got into it, went to the kitchen, grabbed a handful of cookies. Then, at the last minute I remembered I didn't even have the money to get to the airport. I went back into the bedroom and hunted up Nancy's wallet. I took twenty bucks. Then I sat down at her desk and wrote a note saying I'd give the money back

133

to her when I saw her in St. Louis. I wrote down my address and phone number, too. I left the note in her wallet.

Then there wasn't anything else for me to do but go. Still, I just stood there, not wanting to, scared of going, scared of staying. I felt as if I had to jump off a bridge and the only thing I could choose was which side to leap from. Reaching out, I touched the butterfly on Nancy's hand—and then I left.

The doorman got me a taxi, and in a few minutes I was on my way to the airport. Changing the ticket was no problem. The plane took off right on time.

"You had to do it. You had to do it!" was the only thing I said to myself. I must have said it ten million times.

But what I really was thinking was, *Don't worry. She'll be there soon.*

When I got to St. Louis, Aunt Lu and Uncle Carl were waiting for me. I saw them right away. Aunt Lu was waving frantically.

When I got to her she grabbed me, hugged me, kissed me, told me that she forgave me, that everything would be all right, everything was fine, things were going to be good again. Uncle Carl kept patting me on the back, agreeing with her.

I sat in the back seat of the car, and all the way to the house they talked about how glad they were to see me. Not that I listened. I was saying to myself that I had to tell them what had happened. *I had to*.

When we had pulled into the driveway Uncle Carl leaned back and opened the car door for me. "I've got a lovely lunch for you," said Aunt Lu. "All your favorites."

"I want to tell you about it," I said. "What happened." And right there, right then, from the back of the car, I told them the whole story, from beginning to end. All of it. They listened to it all. And they didn't get mad. Aunt Lu didn't cry. They just listened.

Then we went in to lunch, sat down, and ate. No one said a thing until I said, "I'm glad to be home."

It was the best conversation we ever had.

After lunch I went to my room. I think I slept for two days.

And After . . .

My friend Rick came over. "How was England?" he wanted to know. "Did you really see the queen?"

"I went to New York and saw my parents," I said. "My father is selling furniture at Macy's. My mother is a one-person band."

"Is that true?" he said.

"It's true," I told him. And I told him the rest of it, too.

The rest of spring vacation went okay. Mostly I stayed around the house. Everything seemed the same—but we all knew it was different. For one thing, I wasn't taking care of my aunt and uncle anymore. I let them take care of me. It was a lot better.

Most of all, I was waiting for Nancy. I kept making plans for all the things we'd do, the fun we'd have, kept thinking up ways to make her laugh. It would be good for me, too. I could talk to her. I wouldn't have to pretend anything, or fake anything. I mean, she was the most important person of all to me—the one person who really knew what I was and said it was okay.

I knew she would be back on Sunday. So on Monday, I hurried home from school and called the St. Agnes Academy for Girls. Was I excited? It was like I was calling to find out if I had really won a million bucks.

"Can I speak to Nancy Sperling?"

"Who's calling, please?"

"A friend."

"May I have your name, please?"

"Conrad Murray," I said. It felt good just to say my real name.

"One moment, please."

But instead of Nancy's voice, what I heard next was the voice of the same person who had answered the phone. "Mr. Murray, I'll certainly pass on the message, and Miss Sperling can return your call if she wishes. May I have your number, please?"

I told her, and she hung up.

But I didn't get a call.

I went through that business every day. A week went by. I still hadn't heard from Nancy.

I began to get frantic. I *had* to see her. I went to the school. But the guard remembered me, and wouldn't let me go in. When I tried to get past him, he threatened to call the cops.

I was certain she was there, but they wouldn't let her know I was trying to reach her.

Then I got a letter.

Dear Conrad,

I'm not coming back to St. Louis. My parents were terribly angry and upset. They said you were a bad influence on me—and a lot more, worse. None of it is true.

There was a lot of talk. They even made me move upstairs with them.

I never saw Pat get so mad. She stuck up for you. She's mailing this letter for me. I'm not even allowed to write to you.

They are sending me to a school in Switzerland. They say it's a good school, but I don't want to go. I'd rather be in St. Louis near you.

Conrad, every day at five o'clock, your time, we have to think each other's name. Hard. Someone once told me that if two people do that at exactly the same time, their thoughts can connect and they can hear each other—sort of like the arch in St. Louis, the hands reaching up and touching.

Please do it. I love you.

Nancy (your wife)

At the bottom she had drawn a butterfly, a green one.

*   *   *

Just as she asked, I do think her name every day at five. And sometimes I think I hear my name.